I0732054

First edition published 2022 by M.T. Sanders.

Illustrations by Zoe Saunders.

Printed in Great Britain by IngramSparks.

A CIP catalogue record for this book is available from the British Library.

Print Book ISBN - 978-1-7397049-0-2
Ebook ISBN - 978-1-7397049-1-9

DEDICATIONS

This book is dedicated to all dogs everywhere. If making the world a better place makes you a superhero then that's what you all are.

Monty, Cookie, Molly, Poppy and Bailey have enriched our lives and been a huge part of our family for the past 12 years. They have blessed us with K9indness every day and they are the inspiration for this story. I hope you enjoy it.

A massive thank you to all of our family, friends, supporters and followers online and off, that continue to make these stories possible, it would be impossible without your support.

I wanted to say a special mention to two schools who have been amazingly supportive, inviting us back numerous times. A massive thank you to the wonderful staff, children and parents of St Andrew's Church of England Primary School, Rochdale, and Our Lady's R.C. Primary School, Aspull. You have really helped us continue to develop these stories.

As always, a huge thank you to Zoe Saunders not only for the wonderful illustrations but for doing the typesetting of this book

Also, a big shout out to Jane Mosse. Jane jumped in to help with editing and proofreading and that support was invaluable. Thank you.

'NOT EVERYONE CAN BE A SUPERHERO,
BUT WE CAN ALL BE KIND.'

MONTY DOGGE

MIGHTY MONTY
A NEWF KIND OF SUPERHERO

STORY BY
M.T. SANDERS

ILLUSTRATIONS BY
ZOE SAUNDERS

CHAPTER 1
THE FALL

I never wanted to be a superhero. I guess nobody does. I can't imagine that Peter Parker woke up one morning and thought, today seems like a great day to be bitten by a radioactive spider.

So, this was nothing I'd ever thought about. It just happened. And it was a day I'll never forget, that's for sure.

I'd like to say it was just a normal day, but living in our house was never normal. We live in Wigwam and are a large and chaotic household of 5 dogs, 4 hoomans and 4 mini-hoomans. That's not the end of it though; three of the dogs are Cockeared spangles and they make Tigger on a trampoline seem calm.

Molly, Poppy and Bailey never stop. Just watching them makes me feel tired, and they are obsessed with everything. The ball, squirrels, in fact anything that moves or they can rub themselves in or eat. They are certainly a strange bunch and I'd never seen anything like them when I first arrived.

And that brings me round to me. I'm Monty and I'm a Newfydoof. The hoomans call us Newfoundlands but hoomans are strange and don't really know that much. The spangles have shrunk since I arrived. We were about the same size then, but now I'm about ten times bigger. Oh, and I almost forgot, I'm also very handsome and clever.

A few years after I arrived along came Cookie, another

Newfydoof who has become my annoying sister. She enjoys jumping, bouncing and generally trying her best not to let me rest... at all.

Then we have the hoomans and mini-hoomans but they're only there to feed us and pick up our poo, so they aren't really a big part of my story, but I'm sure they will get a mention later.

So, there you have it. That's my family, hooman and dog and there never seems to be anything like a normal day.

The day started as it often did with a walk in the woods. I enjoy a walk like anybody else, but I have to say right now that exercise isn't something that makes me spring out of my nice warm bed for in the morning. To be honest, I don't do springing at all. The spangles on the other hand whine and cry when dad gets the leads out. And when he picks up the ball... well, I often think their little bodies will explode or their big dangly ears will make them take off.

Cookie also like her walks and she often reminds me of a hooge spangle, just with smaller ears. She bounces through the woods like a mahoosive hairy brown bear. I've lost count of the number of unsuspecting walkers she has terrified as she suddenly appears covered in undergrowth and slobber running towards them to say hello, tail wagging like a furry helicopter.

It was a sunny morning as we began our walk and, as usual, I was keeping well away from the others, and just strolled gently through the woods. The spangles were chasing the ball obsessively, and as it flew through the air, they seemed to turn off every bit of sense they have and just focus 100% on where it was going.

As I reached the centre of the woods, there was a gigantic crater covered with undergrowth. I changed direction to avoid it, as it looked very deep. It was just at that point that the spangles headed straight towards the hidden drop and I knew they hadn't seen it because they were chasing the ball. And they are spangles after all.

As they got closer, I shouted to them but while Bailey and Poppy heard me and slowed down Molly was determined to get their first, and took off with a tremendous leap to win the prize. I couldn't just let her fall, so I moved quickly to block her path. It was at this point that I realised how hard a determined spangle in mid-air can hit you. Even though I had an enormous size and weight advantage, Molly's sheer momentum knocked me off my feet and carried us both over the crater's edge and we began falling.

CHAPTER 2
HEAVEN?

The next thing I remember was waking up, and it didn't seem like I was at the bottom of a hole. It was so dazzling I struggled to open my eyes. I was in a brightly lit room with white walls, white ceiling and a white floor. I looked down to see that I was lying on a hooge soft white bed that was raised up off the shiny tiles.

As my eyes adjusted to the glare, I looked across and saw Molly on an identical bed, but just smaller. She was still asleep, and I was just about to get down when the door opened. A dog easily as big as me walked into the room with a clipboard around his neck.

He had a hooge floppy face and when he spoke it was in a deep voice that made him sound important and serious.

'Hello Monty,' he said. 'We've been expecting you.'

Before I had a chance to speak, he said, 'I can see you're confused, I'm sorry I'm sure you want to know where you are.'

I did. 'Is this heav...' But before I could finish, he answered.

'Heaven?' I found myself nodding. 'Not exactly,' he said, 'but you're on the right lines.'

'So...So is this the other pl...'

'Other Place?' he roared with laughter. 'No, no, not at all.'

'I'm not being funny,' I said, 'but do you always finish people's senten...'

'Sentences? Yes, I find it saves time and we have a lot to discuss.'

Well, this didn't feel much like a discussion, but I waited for him to speak again; mainly because I was getting fed up with being interrupted.

'First, let me introduce myself,' he said. 'My name is St...'

'PETER!' I almost shouted – and it felt good to get my own back.

I immediately regretted my comments as he looked sternly down his snout at me. 'If you'll allow me,' he said gruffly.

'My name is St Bernard, and this is my boss, this is DOG.'

Well, I was confused as I hadn't seen anybody, and looked around the room to see if someone had entered without me noticing. As I looked back at St Bernard, he was moving his head down towards the floor.

As I looked down, I saw a small dog. He was black and tan, with tiny little legs, a really long body, and spangle-like floppy ears.

'I'm sorry,' I said. 'I didn't see you down there.'

He didn't seem at all bothered, just stood there with the hint of a smile on his face.

'It's fine.' he said, 'It's nice to meet you. We've been watching you for some time.'

Again, I must have looked confused because DOG's large assistant stepped forward.

'Let me explain, Monty. I know you think you had an accident, but this was in fact planned to get you here as we have something to speak to you about.'

I just nodded, open-mouthed as he spoke. I saw Molly had woken up and was looking even more confused than me.

'Don't worry Molly,' DOG said in a very calming voice. 'All will be explained.'

St Bernard continued with his explanation. 'DOG is in charge of this place, K9HQ, and I assist with most of the day to day running of the operation. We oversee all aspects of dog life and afterlife.'

'So we are de..'

'Dead?' he said, finishing my sentence again.

'No, my dear chap, you're both very much alive. We do manage Rainbow bridge, but this is definitely not your time yet.'

'One of our other roles is superpower distribution, and this is where you come in.'

'Superpower Distribution?' I said, trying not to sound as bewildered as I was feeling.

'Yes,' he continued. 'It's all very subtle and not as dramatic as you see on the TV. We have the guide dogs, rescue dogs, therapy dogs, police and army dogs and even the medical detection dogs. We select dogs from time-to-time who have the right temperament and character to become superhero dogs. How does that sound?'

Well, it sounded crazy, to be honest. At this point I bit my paw, to see if it would wake me up from this dream.

'You're not dreaming Monty,' DOG said as he stepped forward. 'We want to give you a gift, a superpower if you like, because it's our job to make the world a better place for the hoomans.

'I know it's been an enormous shock for you, so take your time. Have a think about what sort of hidden power you'd like and we'll come back when you've had more time. Shall we say five minutes?'

With that DOG left, but just before he followed, St Bernard looked down at his clipboard.

'Just bear in mind Monty.
These powers have already gone...

Invisibility...
Web spinning, obviously.
Turning green and being really strong...
Iron armour coating...

Flying...

Oh, and flames shooting out of your paws.
That never ended well.

Anything else is fine, but choose wisely.

See you shortly,'

And with that he was gone.

As I pictured the superpowers he mentioned, I was quite
pleased they'd already been used.

CHAPTER 3
THE POWER OF K9INDNESS

As soon as the door closed, Molly let out a kind of excited yelp. I looked across at her and asked if she was OK.

'What's going on Monty? Is this real? Am I going to get superpowers too?'

'I'm not really sure Molly, but I've been here a while and haven't woken up yet, so I'm guessing it is.'

'I've heard about this before,' she said.

'You have?' I questioned.

'Yes, yes. There was this Springy spangle I met at the park once and she said they had picked her to sniff for naughty things the hoomans sometimes have and she was going to work for the Pleece. She said they had given her these special powers that meant her nose could smell anything really well and she could find stuff. I remember it because I was thinking how useful it would be when I'm looking for fox poo to roll in.'

'That sounds wonderful Molly,' I said. 'I can see how useful that could be.'

Luckily, before Molly could share any more of her obsessions about anything disgusting to roll in or eat, the door opened and DOG entered, followed by the very official-looking St Bernard.

'I'm sorry we didn't give you much time Monty,' said DOG sincerely.

'No, no it's fine honestly,' and I meant it.

Molly likes to tell stories that go on and on and they are nearly always gross or about the various types of balls she's chased during her lifetime. I know from experience that twenty minutes listening about the benefits of a rubber ball over a tennis ball are twenty minutes of your life you're never getting back.

'The reason we didn't need long is that we feel you already know what superpower you'd like,' he continued.

'I do? Well, that's news to me.' I blurted out before I could even think.

St Bernard let out a big bellowing laugh and DOG gave him an odd sideways look. Clearing his throat, the big dog continued.

'Monty, we've been watching you. We know how you think and what you feel. You've been picked because we already think you're special. Now just close your eyes and think, if you could do anything, what would it be?'

I did what he'd asked and sat in silence for a second.

Next to speak was DOG, he said, 'Just say it out loud Monty, what are you thinking?'

Well, I was actually thinking I was starving and I hoped I hadn't missed dinner, but I guessed that wasn't the answer he was looking for.

'I'd like to make hoomans kinder,' I said.

'Go on...' said DOG, tilting his head with interest.

'Well, I like hoomans and most of them are nice enough,

but I've noticed a lot don't care about others very much. They worry too much about the things they have and that can make some of them very greedy and selfish. Don't get me wrong, there are some lovely hoomans out there, but if they were all kind and caring, then the world would be a much better place. I wish hoomans were more like us, more dog.'

'Hmm,' said DOG thoughtfully as he scratched his left ear. 'It's not exactly what we thought you were going to say, but it's interesting. What do you think, St B?'

He agreed, and then they both shuffled into the corner of the room and began whispering excitedly to each other.

I couldn't hear much other than the occasional 'Yes. Yes.' or 'That could work,' as I sat there wondering what was going to happen next.

'What are they saying?' said Molly. 'What's happening?'

I could see she was trying to talk quietly, but it's very hard for an excited spangle to do anything quietly and I think everyone could hear her.

'I'm not sure,' I said, 'Ssh, just wait.'

'But they haven't asked me yet what superpower I want, do you think they'll ask me next?'

I was just about to answer but DOG and his hooge assistant finished their conversation and came back over to me.

'Can I tell him, boss?' said St Bernard. 'Please, this is a great one.'

'OK,' said DOG in his very calm voice. 'Go ahead.'

'OK, Monty,' said St Bernard. 'We think you've made an excellent choice. Your superpower is a very worthwhile one and you will soon have the ability to give hoomans K9indness.'

'K9indness?' I repeated.

'Yes,' he said, 'K9indness, the simple kindness of a dog. All the things that you said. You can pass that on and they will carry it in their heart forever.'

OK a bit dramatic, I thought, but instead I just said, 'Yeah, sounds great.'

This was a lot to take in.

'It's more than great, Monty, it's genius. This could be the best superpower ever and you are going to be the superhero that delivers it to mankind.'

I think even DOG thought that St Bernard was getting a bit too Hollywood now, and he stepped in front of his enthusiastic second in command.

'OK Monty,' he said. 'We need to just go over the details with you. We won't keep you too long, but we need to bring in our technical expert. Is that OK?'

'That's fine,' I said, not knowing what other option I had, especially as I didn't know where I was or the way out. On top of that, I was about to be given superhero powers by... I didn't know who they were to be honest... so hanging around seemed to be my best option.

'We'll be back,' said St Bernard as they turned to leave.

'Er, excuse me,' said Molly before they reached the door. 'I know we haven't really discussed my superpower yet but

I've been giving it some thought and I think I know what I'd like.'

St Bernard began to answer her. 'Sorry,' he said. 'It's only...' But DOG cut him off.

'It's only Monty was first, is what my assistant was about to say,' and DOG gave St Bernard another of those sideways looks.

'What superpower is it you wanted Molly?'

I could see that the big dog was uncomfortable, but he was obviously outranked here, and he could only stand and listen to the conversation.

'Thank you, Mr DOG,' said Molly. 'I'd really like to have the power to eat anything at all without being sick, and to turn off my hearing when the hoomans are calling me.'

DOG's eyes smiled as he replied, 'Of course Molly, you now have that superpower, use it wisely.'

'Oh, thank you!' said Molly. 'I will!'

With that, DOG turned back to his assistant and just before they left, he winked.

Genius, I thought: that's how you become the boss. You give people the gift they already have.

I looked across at Molly as she sat tail wagging uncontrollably and thought. *This has been the strangest of days.*

CHAPTER 4
F.A.R.T.

We sat for what seemed like hours waiting for... Actually, I'm not sure what we were waiting for, but it seemed a long time anyway.

Luckily, Molly's excitement at her newly acquired 'superpower' meant she didn't want to talk about the size, texture and bounceability of balls. Instead, I marvelled at the very detailed descriptions of the things that she would now be able to sample on our walks. As a bonus, she wouldn't even be able to hear the hoomans calling her back with her new 'mute' setting.

I was pretending I was listening, but instead I was getting a bit anxious about us being missed. I didn't know how long we'd been gone, but my stomach was saying it was nearly tea time, so it had been a while. I was just thinking maybe I should try the door, when it opened.

This time DOG wasn't there, but St Bernard came in, followed by a very attractive yellow-coated dog.

'OK, Monty, I'm going to leave you in the very capable paws of Doctor Gold to go through all the technical details with you. All yours, Doctor.' he said. And with that he turned and left.

'Hello Monty,' she said softly as she walked over, and we touched paws. 'I've heard all about you and this is very exciting.'

'You h–have?' I stuttered, suddenly feeling a little warm.

'Yes,' she said, 'but where are my manners? Would you like some water, you're panting?'

'I'm fine,' I replied, 'I'm just a little warm, but it's OK, you carry on.'

'OK then,' she said. 'I'm Dr Gold, and I'm the head of Lab technical services – Canine Division. This means I work on all the superpowers given to dogs across the whole planet.'

'Impressive,' I said, looking into her large brown eyes. 'The whole planet, eh?'

I was hoping to say something more intelligent, but that's all that came out and I wondered why I was finding it hard to put two sensible words together.

'Yes, and this is really exciting, because you are the first dog ever to be given this particular gift, and we have been working for quite a while on the delivery mechanism.'

'The delivery mechanism?' I repeated, and now I started feeling like some hooge silly parrot repeating words and making no sense at all.

'Yes,' she continued. 'K9indness needs to get to the hooman in question from the host, our superhero, YOU. We needed to find a way to make this happen that doesn't attract too much attention so it needs to be invisible and silent.'

'That doesn't sound like it's going to be easy,' I said.

'No,' it's certainly had its challenges,' she replied, 'but we think we have it perfected now. You will be able to pass the wonderful K9indness to any hooman you choose unnoticed, through our newly developed Fast Air Release

Tool or F.A.R.T. for short.'

As she finished talking, I looked over at her to see if she was laughing as surely this must be a joke. No. Her face was deadly serious.

'So, the Fast Air Release Tool, is…is…' I was struggling to get my words out and she must have seen my difficulties as she explained further, even though I wasn't sure I wanted her to.

'The Fast Air Release Tool will emit a rapid stream of k9indness particles from the host's rear end assisted by an enhanced tail blast.'

'OK, I think I'm clear,' I said.

Suddenly, the events of the day seemed to tumble down on me like the left overs on a plate when you try to sneak it from the counter. It was at this point that DOG and his trusty right-pawed assistant came back into the room.

'Everything OK?' said the St Bernard. 'Are you understanding the technical aspects, Monty? Do you think he's good-to-go Doctor?'

She nodded, and began to speak about teething problems and prototypes, but my mind was spinning.

When she'd finished, I said, 'So let me get this clear and please correct me if I'm wrong. Feel free to jump in at any point.'

I looked over at St Bernard as I spoke, who just stood there with his massive tongue hanging out, drooling slightly from the corner of his mouth.

I continued, 'I'd been for a stroll in the woods, when all

of a sudden I fell down a hooge hole while trying to save Molly from suffering that same fate… After the fall we both woke up in the whitest and brightest room I'd ever seen. It was at that point that we were joined by your good selves, who explained to me that I had been selected to become a superhero with special powers that would help mankind. This would entail me firing particles of K9indness at mean hoomans out of my backside with an advanced technique called F.A.R.T. Have I missed anything?'

The three all looked at each other nodding in agreement and St Bernard let out a hooge bellowing laugh.

'No that's it Monty. I think you've got it all there.'

DOG then stepped forward and said, 'I know it's been a long day and there's a lot to take in, but it will all become clear over the next few days. Dr Gold will be here at all times for you to get in touch with for any problems you may have, particularly in the early days.'

We looked at each other as she spoke.

'That's right Monty, I'll be here for you. I think we work well together don't you?'

I did, and that did make me feel better.

Chapter 5
What's My Name?

'Right,' said St Bernard. 'We just have the contract to go through and we need to think of a name.'

'A name?' I said, with some confusion. 'I already have a name; it's Monty – remember?'

'No, your Superhero name. You need to have a superhero name,' replied the big dog. 'Well, actually it's mainly for branding and copyright purposes, you understand, but yes, you do need one,' said DOG, very officially.

'What about Farty Monty?' said Molly, chuckling to herself with obvious amusement.

'I don't think that's the kind of thing we're looking for Molly,' said DOG, clearing his throat and giving her a stern look down his thin, long snout.

'I'm not sure,' I said, 'I haven't really thought about it.'

'Well, it's a good job we have then,' said DOG's ever vocal assistant.

'There's F.A.R.T. Dog...'

I think my face must have answered that suggestion pretty clearly, as he quickly moved on.

'Err OK... How about SuperF.A.R.T.er?'

'Seriously?' I said, 'Do we have to mention the FART word in all of the names?'

'No,' he replied. 'OK then... How about Captain UK?'

'I think we could have some legal issues with the guys at Marvel if we use that one,' said DOG.

'OK. How about, Captain Monty, Captain Newfydoof, Colonel Monty? Let's outrank them.' The big dog laughed at his own joke, and also laughed by himself.

'How about Captain Kindness?' It was the first time Dr Gold had spoken. 'I think that suits Monty really well.'

We smiled at each other. 'I quite like that.' I said.

DOG walked forward and got all of our attention instantly, as was his way. 'I think we should steer clear of Captain or Colonel or any ranks for that matter, and concentrate on our own ideas. I like Mighty Monty.'

We all looked at each other, and there seemed to be an agreement.

'That has a ring to it for sure,' said St Bernard.'I think that's the one. What do you think Monty?'

'Yes,' I said, 'I quite like that one.'

To be honest at this point I think I would have been happy with anything, I just wanted to get home for dinner.

'That's it then,' said DOG with a tone of finality. 'St Bernard, can you draw up the contract, please?'

'Does he get a costume?' asked Molly, as DOG turned to leave.

'No, I don't think so,' he said. 'This needs to be a low-profile operation, so I think Monty needs to be in plain fur for this. We may be able to organise a bib. I'll leave that with you St B.'

With that he left, and St Bernard followed soon after to organise the contract.

When he returned a little while later, the Doctor left. I watched as she walked away, and St Bernard said to me reassuringly, 'She'll be back in a while, Monty. She has to go through the final bits with you. Now, you just need to have a quick read through this and I'll be done.' He rolled out the contract on the floor so that I could read it.

'It's all pretty basic stuff,' he said, 'K9indness and F.A.R.T. remain the intellectual property of K9HQ Ltd, and said items can only be used by bone-a-fied Superheroes in the employ of said organisation bla bla bla. I'm sure you get the picture. Now if I could just have your pawtagraph here, and here.'

As he said that, he pointed at two places on the paper and produced an ink pad. I pressed my paw onto the pad and then pressed down on the contract.

'Excellent!' he roared in his deep, raspy voice. 'That's me done. Good luck and don't forget we're here anytime for any questions you may have. Doctor Gold will go through all the aftercare and tech support with you when she...'

At that point she entered the room flanked by two smaller dogs each carrying a container.

'Great timing Doctor,' said St Bernard. 'I'm all done here, they're all yours.'

With that, he left without a backwards glance and the door closed behind him.

'OK,' said the Doctor. 'Here, we have the superpower

implants for you. It's all very painless, just like when you go to the vetandhairyman for your jab.'

The two assistants opened the containers and first took one marked 'Placebo' and jabbed it gently into Molly's neck using their mouth.

'Wow,' I said, 'that's clever.'

'They are highly trained specialists Monty, but you may need to lie down for them to reach your neck.' I did as she asked.

'What's *Pler Cee Do*?' asked Molly, trying to say the word correctly and failing.

'Ah, that's just its technical name.' replied the Doctor. 'Nothing for you to worry about Molly.'

Molly seemed content with the answer and lay back down. Then the second assistant injected me with the syringe from the other container.

'Excellent!' said Doctor Gold. She turned to the assistants and thanked them. They took the empty containers and left.

'We're nearly done and then you two can get back home,' said the Doctor, 'just a few more things to go through. The Superpower implant becomes live in 12 hours, Monty, and you will then notice a change. Yours is a fast acting one Molly and is working now.'

'What kind of change?' I asked hesitantly as I remembered how this was going to be delivered, and pictured in my mind the kind of changes that may begin to happen.

'Don't worry, Monty, the changes will be subtle. The F.A.R.T.

system will deploy the K9indness when you choose and this may take a bit of practice. Remember, you can't affect people who are already kind, so practicing isn't going to be a problem. On top of the F.A.R.T. we have given you some additional tail swishiness to help with aim, and we have tweaked your hearing to allow you to identify worthwhile recipients of K9indness.

'Now remember,' she continued, 'you can come back at any point if there are any problems or you have any queries. There may be some teething troubles to start with, but I'm not expecting too much. All you need to do is come back to the large oak tree, and the door will appear for you. You'll then arrive back here and I'll be waiting.'

'Thank you, Doctor,' I said. 'That is really good to know.'

'It's really no trouble Monty, we have to look after our superheroes, and you can call me Honey.' She pointed behind me with her paw as she spoke. 'This door is the way back home; all you need to do is follow the corridor and go through the door at the end. You'll then be back and everything will be back to...well, almost normal.'

I don't know how long we'd been in the room, but I had seen no other door at all. But as she pointed it out, there it was. It was slightly open and Molly and I said goodbye and entered into the corridor. As we went through the door, it closed behind us and suddenly became just a wall. The only way was forward, and we walked slowly along the brightly lit passageway.

As she had told us we would, we eventually came to a door. We pushed against it, and it opened. We tumbled out into the woodland. As I looked behind me, the door seemed to merge into the trees until it was invisible.

 Molly looked at me and I just said, 'Come on Molly, let's go home.'

CHAPTER 6
HOME AGAIN

As we walked through the woods, I think we were both thinking the same thing. It was confirmed when Molly turned to me and said, 'Did that really happen, Monty, or was it a dream?'

I really wasn't sure, but how could we both have had the same dream?

'I'm not sure Molly, but I think we'll find out soon enough.'

Up ahead, we saw the tree-circled crater where all this had started. Standing around the edge were Bailey, Poppy, Cookie and Dad; all staring down into the hole. They didn't notice us as we walked up and stood next to them.

'What are we looking at?' I said.

They all turned together and looked at Molly and me as if we were something from another planet.

'Where have you been?' said Dad. 'We were sure you'd gone down this hole... Oh well, never mind, at least you're both safe.' He smiled and then said, 'Come on, let's get home, it's time for dinner.'

Later that night, after we'd eaten, and the hoomans were watching the TV, Molly gathered everyone around to tell them what had happened to us. She spoke really fast as she excitedly recalled everything that had happened.

I could see the others looking at each other with a hooge amount of disbelief, and I don't blame them. I was struggling to think it was real, and I was there. When she finished, there was an awkward silence as nobody seemed to know what to say next.

'So,' said Bailey after a few minutes, 'Monty, you're a superhero and have the power to give K9indness to nasty hoomans?'

I nodded. 'Yes, that seems to be the general idea. They said they'd been watching me for a while and thought I'd be perfect.'

'OK then, show us.' said Bailey, and they all looked at me, obviously waiting for something amazing to happen.

'I can't,' I said. 'First of all, it doesn't work for 12 hours, and second, you already have the K9indness – so you wouldn't be able to see any difference.'

I could see the doubt on their faces that any of this was in fact real. Again, I couldn't blame them because the whole thing sounded like a big practical joke. They looked as if they thought Molly and me would burst out laughing at any moment and tell them we'd made it all up.

'My superpower is working now though.' said Molly, and they all turned round to look at her. 'But I don't think I can use it at this precise moment, because I've just eaten, and the hoomans are in there watching TV.'

'So, what's your Soo Perrr Powww Errr then Molly?' Cookie spoke sarcastically to her small dog-sis. I think they'd all had enough of the story now and it didn't get any better when Molly replied.

'I have the power to eat anything without being sick, and I

can turn off my hearing when the hoomans call me.'

Cookie, Bailey and Poppy all looked at each other, and this time it was Poppy that spoke. 'But Molly, you're a spangle, you alr...'

'OK,' I said quickly before Poppy could finish her sentence. 'I think we should carry this on in the morning. It's been a long day and I, for one, am exhausted.'

With that, we all went for our last toilet break of the day and settled down to a good night's sleep. As I drifted off, I could still hear Cookie, Bailey and Poppy whispering to themselves. I couldn't help but wonder what tomorrow would bring.

Chapter 7
Miss Fothergill

Miss Fothergill lived on our estate. She was well known by everyone locally, as she had probably upset them all at some point over the years. She had lived in the same house since she was born, and felt that this alone gave her an elevated position in the community. I think it's fair to say she wasn't very popular because of her manner, but she had a particular loathing for Cookie and me.

She lived alone, apart from three tiny Pomeranian dogs that were unlucky enough to share her house. She was just mean; she was mean to everyone she met, and even to her poor dogs.

We saw her regularly as she was out dragging her dogs around the estate. She constantly remarked about our size and fur and what awful slobbery beasts we were. Dad always tried to keep away as much as he could, but it wasn't always possible and he nearly always ended up being chastised by her for one thing or another.

As we were eating breakfast in the morning, I could still feel the other dogs looking at us, waiting for something or more like nothing to happen. I felt no different, but I wasn't sure how I'd feel when my powers started, so I was really none the wiser; until I went out into the garden.

As I was having a sniff around the flowerbed, I heard two hoomans talking. They sounded close and so I immediately went into stranger alert mode and looked to see where they were. Nothing! There was nobody in the garden. I looked everywhere, even behind the shed, but the garden was completely empty.

Then I heard them again, and this time they seemed closer. Again, I looked but nobody was there, and then I suddenly spotted them. They were in their garden...at the end of the street. But I could hear them like they were right next to me, and then I remembered what Doctor Gold, er Honey, had said to me.

'And we have tweaked your hearing to allow you to identify worthwhile recipients of K9indness.'

That must be it. It was working. I had superpowers. I was Mighty Monty. I could hear the hoomans like they were standing next to me. This was going to be fun! I thought, and I ran back into the house to tell the others.

When it was time for our walk, I must admit I was very excited. I wanted to see what else would happen. Sometimes we walked with Dad around the estate, but most days we just went over into the woods and fields that backed onto our house.

Today it was a lead walk, and Poobag came with us. Poobag was Dad's mini-hooman, but she had grown up, and had her own mini-hoomans. Are you lost yet? Imagine how we feel; we're just dogs. I don't think Poobag is her real name, but it's what Dad always used to say to her when we were pups and it kind of stuck, much to her delight.

So, Dad, Poobag, and the five of us all set out for our walk on this bright spring day. The expectancy of this newly-acquired super power was making my heart pound as we turned out of our road and headed up towards the church.

I don't know if it was fate that meant that Miss Fothergill was out walking at the same time as us today, but I certainly heard her before I saw her.

Her shrill voice combined with my new enhanced hearing meant that even at a distance, her presence was almost painful. Not everyone had the advantage of an early warning though and unfortunately for Dad, as he turned the corner, he came face to face with her.

It was like a wild-west standoff for about a nano second, until all of a sudden, the Pomeranians exploded with excitement, or maybe it was fear. They started yapping constantly while frantically spinning around on their leads like furry ballerinas, as their scowling hooman began losing the fight to control them.

The spangles, never ones to refuse an invite to a crazy-party, joined in; almost mimicking the three smaller dogs by barking and spinning around. Poobag was also struggling to get anywhere near control, as now six swirling balls of fur became more and more entangled with each other.

'Get them off!' said Miss Fothergill, as she attempted unsuccessfully to separate her three pups from the spangles. 'Get your animals under control!' she screamed. As she continued with her verbal barrage of insults, she also lashed out with her foot, attempting to kick Molly, Poppy and Bailey.

Dad, up until this point, had stood back with Cookie and I, but as soon as the spangles came under attack from this awful hooman, Cookie decided it was time to act. She dragged Dad across the pavement and got between the attacker and the three victims of her outburst.

Cookie pushed against Miss Fothergill with her snout, to stop her moving forward. This had the double effect of halting the attack and coating the snooty woman's smart walking jacket with slobber.

'Get off me, you disgusting beast!' she screamed, as she saw the slimy shoelaces hanging from her clothes. She swung her handbag and connected with Cookie square on the top of her head, and at this point Dad joined in with the mayhem.

'Excuse me,' he said, much politely than I'd been expecting. 'Please stop hitting my dogs or...'

'OR WHAT?!' she screamed, her face turning redder by the second. 'OR WHAT?!'

'Or there is going to be trouble.' said Dad, as he tried to restore some sense of order.

'HA!' she said indigently, as she aimed a kick at Bailey, which luckily missed.

I had been watching the events, somewhat stunned that anybody could behave like this. Her poor dogs were now cowering as she continued to scream. They must see this all the time.

This hooman needs to change.

If there was ever a time to try out my new power, this seemed the perfect moment. How does it work though? I hadn't even had a trial run. I moved round the side of Dad and positioned myself facing away from the wailing hoomans and just concentrated. I'd like some K9indess for this person.

WHOOSH!

I felt a rush of air and my tail wagged wildly. I turned to look at Miss Fothergill, waiting for her mood to change. I watched and nothing. She continued to shout and swing her bag at everyone within reach.

Then suddenly something changed. She stopped and looked confused. 'Oh my...' she said, 'Oh my, I feel strange.'

It was working.

This was it; she was going to become kind, I'd done it.

But just at that moment she staggered across the pavement. 'I feel faint...' she said in a weak voice. The words had hardly left her mouth when she spun round and fell head first into a large bush that was in a garden next to the path.

Everyone watched in disbelief. It was almost like slow motion before the mayhem started again. Now there were people coming out of their houses as they heard and saw the commotion. The three Pomeranians, now released from the grip of their hooman ran around the gardens and road, leads trailing behind them.

Miss Fothergill was still head first in the bush, legs pointing to the sky, and her very large frilly knickers on show to the world. Some hoomans were trying to pull her out to save any further embarrassment, while others gave her first aid.

Eventually, her dogs were rounded up, and an ambulance arrived. As soon as everything had calmed down, Dad and Poobag turned back and headed home. They obviously thought we'd had enough excitement for the day, but I couldn't get my mind off the events.

Had I made that happen? Surely this wasn't the way my new superpower was meant to work? I wanted to give people K9indness; not hurt them.

I needed to find out why this had happened and fast.

Once we got home and the hoomans were occupied, I slipped out of the back and headed across the fields towards the woods.

I needed to get to the bottom of this. I needed some answers.

Chapter 8
Looking for Answers

When I arrived at the woods, I headed for the large oak tree where Honey had said to return to for help. There was no door, I walked round three or four times but it definitely wasn't there. Maybe this was all a dream. Maybe that hooman had just got herself so angry that she just fainted and it was nothing to do with me.

I was just about to give up and head home when I heard a creak. As I turned round, I saw that the door had appeared. It was slightly ajar, and I saw a bright light coming from inside.

As I squeezed through the opening, I was back inside the familiar corridor and I headed down towards the far end. Sure enough, there was the door, and as I pushed through, I was back in the room where all this began. Now hopefully I could find out what had gone wrong with my first attempt to be Mighty Monty.

I had literally just entered the room when Honey Gold entered, flanked by the two assistants who had given us the jabs. Before I could say a word, she spoke.

'Monty, I'm so sorry. We have had the information back already from the automatic reporting system that is built into F.A.R.T. There has been an error, and we are devastated. Let me assure you this has never happened before.'

'Go on,' I said. 'So what went wrong?'

'Well,' she replied. 'Somebody seems to have made an error with the K9indness module and given you something different instead.' As she spoke, she glanced across at one of her assistants, who looked down at her paws. 'We have been working on a way to allow Police dogs to stop somebody acting really nastily without having to bite them all the time. They do have some concerns about catching something from these hoomans you see; so we have developed STOPnSLEEP. It seems that this is what you gave to that nasty hooman this morning.'

She continued, 'On a positive note Monty, it does seem to work well, and you did stop her causing any more trouble.'

She quickly stopped smiling when she saw I wasn't too happy that I'd zapped a neighbour with a law enforcement grade weapon.

'Like I said, Monty, we're really sorry, but we have worked out the removal and addition implant and this will now give you the K9indness module that we'd agreed.'

'OK,' I said. 'Don't worry about it, it's just one of those things, I guess mistakes happen.' I felt sorry for the assistant who'd made the mistake. I didn't want them to get into trouble because of me. Everyone can mess up and after all I live with hoomans and they are always doing stupid stuff.

'Thank you Monty, I promise we have it right this time and if you're OK, we'll get you jabbed and you can get back.'

I nodded, and the other assistant came over and gave me the injection.

'That's it then,' said Honey. 'You're free to go Monty, and

apologies again for the error we're not usually like this.'

I reassured her again as I left. 'Hope to see you soon Doctor Gold... err, Honey.'

And with that, I left and headed back out into the woods.

When I got back home, all of the talk was about the day's events. Dad and Poobag were still telling Mum everything that had happened. I could hear bits of the conversation as I came in through the back door.

'...And then she just kind of passed out.'

'...It was like somebody had given her a sleeping potion.'

I felt guilty as I heard the discussions but hopefully that was the end of it now.

I'd hoped too soon, because as soon as the other dogs saw me, they all came over and surrounded me.

'What happened Monty? 'Molly was first to speak. 'Was that the K9indness? I didn't think it would make people fall over like that.'

Before I could answer, Cookie joined in. 'It was great Monty. She was trying to hit me one moment and then she was diving into the hedge head first.'

They all laughed, but I stopped them.

'Look, that wasn't meant to happen. I know Miss Fothergill isn't very nice, but I don't want to be hurting anyone.' I explained the mistake to them and that it had all now been sorted. 'So that's it, that's the end of it. Now let's forget about it and pretend it never happened.'

Well, that would have been the ideal situation, but whilst

I was happy to hear no more about it, these thoughts
weren't shared by a certain disgruntled lady.

CHAPTER 9
SHE'S BACK

That evening, as I lay out in my usual position by the front door, I heard an unmistakable shrill voice. I was beginning to regret the new super-hearing I'd been given, because it was at times like this I'd have rather not been hearing what I was.

The first voice was Miss Fothergill's there was no doubt, and she was obviously still furious.

'I will not calm down and I'd thank you to just do your job officer!'

The second voice was a lot calmer and was obviously trying to keep some order.

'Look, madam, we are simply here to follow up on your report. Let's try to keep things civil.'

The heated discussion was still going on as there was a knock at the door and it was obviously no surprise to me when Dad opened the door to find Miss Fothergill and a police officer on the door step.

'Don't call me Madam...' she said continuing her rant, seemingly oblivious to the fact that Dad was now standing there. 'And civil wasn't how things were this morning. In fact, it was far from civil and it's all his fault!'

She spun round and pointed directly at Dad, who hadn't yet even had a chance to say a word. He looked shocked. 'Him and his awful dogs!' she looked down at me with a glare that could have cracked a mirror.

At this point, the officer who was struggling to keep his composure attempted to bring the situation under control. He looked at Dad.

'Sir, we have had a complaint from a local resident...er Miss Fothergill,' he said as he realised there was no point trying to keep her anonymous. He continued. 'She states she was assaulted, and that your dogs were dangerously out of control.'

'YES!' she screamed in my dad's face, 'Dangerous! That's what they are... DAN- GER-OUS!'

'Now Miss Fothergill,' said the officer, 'If you don't calm down, I am going to have to ask you to leave and that will delay our investigation.' That seemed to do the trick, and she reluctantly took a step back.

He turned back to Dad, who still looked in a state of bewilderment, and spoke again. 'It is alleged that this morning whilst out walking her dogs Miss Fothergill became involved in an altercation with yourself and another person. It was at this point your dogs became involved and that resulted in the lady in question to be rendered unconscious.'

'It FARTED at me. That one there. It just came at me, and it farted. Oh, it was awful. The next thing I knew I was waking up in hospital so they must have attacked me as well.'

I saw Dad and the officer look at each other, and then the officer looked back at Miss Fothergill. 'Please Ma..er... Miss Fothergill, please can I remind you to let me handle this.' She crossed her arms haughtily and stopped speaking.

Finally, Dad got a chance to say something, and looked at the officer. 'Obviously I'm pleased to see that Miss Fothergill has recovered after her accident, but I can categorically say that the altercation was not started by us and there was absolutely no threat by any of my dogs. And as for one of them farting at her... Well, that's just ridiculous.'

That was it. There was no stopping her now.

'RIDICULOUS?!' she screamed. 'RIDICULOUS?! What's ridiculous is that this man hasn't been arrested yet, and his dogs are still free. They are a menace to society. A MENACE I tell you!'

She was frantically waving her arms and getting redder and redder in the face.

'I want this, this, vulgar person,' she pointed at Dad, 'and his stinky dog arrested. NOW!'

To be honest, I'd known for the past few minutes what I had to do, but the memory of this morning was weighing on my mind. Honey's words kept coming back to me...

'This will give you the K9indness module that we'd agreed.'

I had to trust her. I had to believe in myself. I had to be Mighty Monty.

Nobody saw me as I stood up. Everyone was too distracted by the crimson-faced, arm-swirling crazy lady to notice me backing slowly towards the open door.

This time it was easier, and I felt the blast of, hopefully, the right ingredient. The gas floated towards Miss Fothergill and the officer, and my tail helped it on its way. I turned slowly and nervously to see the impact. What if it went wrong again, and this time I also sent a policeman to sleep? That would be bad. That would be very bad.

I was going through all the possible scenarios when, all of a sudden, it went quiet. Both Miss Fothergill and the officer looked confused for a second, and it was obvious something was happening. They both coughed simultaneously.

The officer then looked at Dad and said, 'We have to take these allegations seriously sir, and I have to tell you at this point there could be further action depending on our investigations.'

Dad was just about to reply when Miss Fothergill spoke instead. 'What allegations, officer? What were we talking about again?'

'Well… your allegations, madam.' The policeman sounded confused. 'Your report stated that you were attacked by these people and their dogs and…'

He never got a chance to finish.

'Attacked? By this wonderful family and their amazing dogs? Officer, this couldn't be further from the truth. I had a nasty turn and fainted and these marvellous people were there to help me.'

'But, but', said the confused officer. 'You said…'

'Oh stop talking nonsense officer, you obviously weren't listening. I came round to thank these good folk for their help, and now I think it's time to leave them in peace. Goodnight.'

With that, she turned and left, leaving a very confused police officer standing on the doorstep alone. 'Er, well, that's that then,' he said, his words stumbling as they left his mouth. 'I'm very sorry to have bothered you. Goodnight.'

Dad said goodnight to the officer and closed the door. As we turned around, everyone was gathered there, obviously drawn by the commotion. Dad went off with mum and Poobag and I could hear him trying to explain. 'It must have been the bump on the head,' he said. 'It can do strange things sometimes. At least that's the end of it and she seemed almost pleasant for a minute there.'

I went into the kitchen, and the others followed.

'It worked!' said Molly.

'Yes, you did it!' agreed Bailey.

I was still a bit stunned, but I had to go along with them. 'Yes,' I said. 'I think I gave her the K9indness.'

And it turned out that I really had.

Miss Fothergill became a wonderful neighbour and member of the community. She opened a Pomeranian rescue from her house, which took in all those dogs that didn't have a home. Eventually it became a rescue for all breeds, as Miss Fothergill could never turn away an animal in need.

So popular was she and her efforts, that local mini hoomans came round to help her and take the little dogs for walks. We saw her from time to time and she was always really pleasant, waving and smiling to us.

It seems this time I'd got it right.

CHAPTER 10
LORD DEVLIN

Growler opened his eyes and shuffled on the dirty sack he had spent the night on. The cold of the barn floor came up through the thin bed and chilled his body. He had been woken up suddenly by the sound of his name being called from the house.

'Growler! Get here now, there's work to be done.'

The large Akita reluctantly left the barn and headed across the courtyard towards the house. Inside, Lord Devlin paced impatiently across the kitchen floor as he waited for the dog to come to his command.

He had lived in the house at Douglas Manor his whole life. It had been passed down to him along with his title, which gave him some considerable influence in the local community. However, he was not a popular man, and was seen by many as cruel and uncaring.

He made his money by hunting and shooting, and charged large amounts to those who wanted to take part in the often-illegal activity. Though fox hunting had been banned for many years, Lord Devlin still actively organised hunts and kept the authorities away by pretending the hounds were simply following a scent trail.

Growler had become Lord Devlin's enforcer with the hounds. Often, they were reluctant to hunt the foxes, so they were threatened with no food, water or shelter. Growler was given the job as messenger for the unkind hooman.

He had lived with the Lord since he was asked to leave K9HQ, where he had been a superhero dog a few years previously. He had been given the power of being able to talk to hoomans through a mechanism called 'thought transfer'. They hoped this would help many animals who were unable to say what was wrong with them when they were unwell or in pain.

It had gone badly wrong though, because Growler had told a hooman all about the inner workings and secrets of K9HQ for the promise of treats. It was quickly decided that communicating with hoomans would never work because there were lots of untrustworthy ones. Hoomans understanding the power of dogs could not be risked, so they told Growler that his powers were to be taken away.

Growler left vowing never to return, and that's when he moved into his new home with the Lord and his unsavoury staff, Bob Grimly and Stanley Gough.

Lord Devlin had taken him in, knowing what had happened and the fallout with K9HQ. He thought the big dog could be very useful to him in the future. He had plans and Growler would help him, whether he wanted to or not.

CHAPTER 11
THE CON TRICK

Life returned to normal after the incident with Miss Fothergill and we went back to our routine of walks, naps, and snacks. Although Molly, Poppy, Bailey and Cookie all knew about my newly-gained superpowers, the hoomans were still oblivious.

This was a good thing, as generally we like to keep knowledge of our dog world away from the hoomans. It's not that we don't like them, but just that they don't really understand stuff very well, and it usually makes things complicated. It's just easier if we keep our world to ourselves, and this was definitely the case with these new abilities. They really wouldn't get it.

My next Mighty Monty experience was as unexpected as the first, but once again started by something I heard. The new hearing tweaks which had been added in my return trip to K9HQ seemed to have improved things. Now it only switched on when there was some conflict or nasty behaviour going on. This was much better, as I didn't hear every conversation that was within 100 metres or so.

So when I heard two hooman men talking from a distance away I immediately knew I needed to hear it. I went out through the back garden and headed towards where the conversation was coming from. As I turned the corner of the next street from ours, I saw them standing on the roof of a house.

They were both wearing bright yellow jackets like workmen. The Slater brothers were local and were well known to most of the town's police officers.

Barry Slater was the elder of the two. He was a short, squat man with a big belly that bulged underneath his clothes. He wore a woolly hat and had a deep, raspy voice. The younger brother was Darren. Darren Slater was tall with long, greasy hair that he kept pushing back as it fell across his face. He had a wispy beard and a bad tattoo of a lion on the side of his neck.

The two men were pulling at something, and I heard Darren as he turned to speak to Barry. 'There's not much wrong here Baz, but if we make a couple of holes we should be OK for a few quid.' He spoke quietly, as if he didn't want to be overheard. How could he know I was picking up everything with my sooper-dooper hearing skills?

Barry spoke next. 'He looks like he may have money tucked away somewhere. These old uns always seem to have some.' They both sniggered and continued pulling at the roof.

I had heard Dad talking about hoomans like these. They go round and tell people they have noticed their roof is damaged and it needs fixing. It doesn't really but they do it mainly to the older hoomans who can't climb up a ladder to see for themselves. From what they were saying I was sure these were the very same ones. I needed to do something.

The problem for me was the fact that they were on the

roof, and I was never going to be able to climb a ladder. Even my extra swooshie tail would never be enough to get the K9indness up that high, so I needed to think of something else.

As I stood just outside the garden at the bottom of the drive one of them spotted me. 'Hey Daz look at that thing!' He pointed at me as he spoke. 'Flipping heck that's a beast! Hope it's had breakfast!'

They both laughed, and I realised I needed to get out of sight so I didn't mess up my plans. I don't know who they thought they were calling a 'thing' and a 'beast' but I disliked them even more now, and it made me more determined to help their poor victims.

I moved away, still trying to work out how to get over the ladder problem, when I spotted what I thought must be their van. It was parked outside the house, and it seemed to be held together only by the dirt and rust that covered it. On the top was a place to keep ladders. I felt almost certain that this belonged to the two nasty hoomans who were up on the roof.

As I walked round the side, the door was slightly open. This could be my chance I thought, and as I nudged it with my nose, a bigger gap appeared. It was just big enough for me to squeeze through, and I climbed quietly into the back of the van. In here it was as dirty as the outside, and there were old paint tins and rusty tools everywhere.

Now I was in here I needed to work out some kind of plan, so I looked around to see if there was anything that might help.

CHAPTER 12
A PLAN IS HATCHED

The elderly hooman that lived in the house had come outside and was standing at the bottom of the ladders.

'Everything OK?' He shouted, trying to see where the two men were. 'Would you lads like a cuppa? My wife has just put the kettle on.'

Barry came to the top of the ladder and shouted back down.

'Yes, milk and sugar for both of us. This is worse than we thought up here; it could take a while.'

With that, he moved back out of sight. 'Gimmee a shout when it's done and I'll send the lad down,' he yelled as he went. The old man returned to the house where his wife was making the drinks in the kitchen.

He sounded worried as he spoke. 'The fella says it looks bad and it could take a while to fix.'

'Oh, I hope it isn't going to be expensive,' she said, sounding very concerned. 'We only have a little bit in our savings account, and I was trying to put a little aside for the grandchildren's Christmas presents.'

'Well, the roof needs fixing dear,' he said. 'We can't have it leaking, can we?'

He carried the drinks outside and called up to the men. Darren soon appeared and came down the ladder. 'Thanks Pops,' he said, as he took the drinks from the elderly man.

'Your roof is a right mess. Good job we spotted it from the road. This could have been a disaster – water everywhere. You'd have been flooded out.' He went back up the ladder with the drinks, quietly sniggering to himself.

The old man went back into the house, his shoulders slumped with obvious concern at the latest update. On the roof Darren laughed as he told his partner in crime what he'd said.

'I told him there was loads of damage up here. What's he going to do? He's hardly coming up the ladder to look, is he?'

Barry agreed. 'Nah, he'll just believe what we say and pay up. I think this could be worth a couple of grand if we play our cards right.' They both laughed as they sat drinking their tea and plotted their next move.

I heard everything from inside the van. I was desperate to help the elderly hoomans if I could and I think I had a plan. I had found an old sheet in the back and managed to get myself underneath and out of sight. Now it was just a matter of waiting.

From my hiding position, I heard the old man speaking to his wife. 'It sounds expensive dear, but at least these nice lads spotted it and are going to fix it for us.' She sounded sad as she replied; 'Yes, it is. I'll check our savings but we don't have too much left now after paying our bills.'

'Don't worry love,' he reassured her, they won't charge any more than they need to, I'm sure. They seem like a lovely couple of fellas.'

Back on the roof, the plan took on more detail as the two

brothers plotted how best to take advantage of the two pensioners.

'OK', said Barry. 'Here's what we'll do. We'll go down and tell them that we have to go and get supplies to fix the roof. I'll tell him it'll cost one and a half grand, and then we can offer them a little discount for cash so they think we're giving them a good deal.' He laughed, and Darren joined in.

'Then we'll go to the café and get some breakfast. Once we've finished, we can come back, grab a few things we've got lying about in the van, then get back up here and fix this bit of damage we did.' He smiled as he thought what an easy pay-day this would be.

'Genius,' said Darren, and pulled a bit more of the felt away just in case anybody was to come up on the roof. I heard everything, and it made me really angry. I was more determined than ever to do something, and it was time for Mighty Monty to save the day. And I waited.

The men came down the ladder and knocked on the back door. Darren handed the cups over when the door opened. Barry then stepped forward and spoke to the homeowners.

'We're off to get some supplies because this needs fixing as soon as possible. It's a mess up there.'

'OK,' replied the elderly man. 'Thank you.'

'We'll be back soon and we've worked out the price. It will be one thousand five hundred pounds.' He let the news sink in before he continued. 'Because we only take cash and as you're such nice people, we're going to give you a two-hundred-pound discount. How does that sound?'

The couple looked at each other, obviously distressed, but when the man spoke he sounded grateful. 'Well, that's very kind of you both. Thank you.'

'Great,' said Barry, 'We'll need it at the end of the job this afternoon, we'll be back soon. See ya.'

With that, they turned and headed towards the van. The couple went back in the house, but I could still hear them.

'That's all we have in the world Len,' said the elderly lady.

'I know love, but we have to have the roof fixed, it's really important.'

'Maybe we should get a second opinion,' she said. 'There may be people willing to fix it more cheaply.'

'Cheaper isn't always better,' he replied. 'And plus, in the meantime, if we got a lot of rain we could get flooded. Best just sort it out now while these lads are here.'

He didn't like to go back on his word and he had told them to go ahead and so now he felt it was the right thing to do.

CHAPTER 13
A CHANGE OF HEART

As the two hoomans got into the van, I didn't move a muscle. The sheet hid me and they got straight into the front seats, not looking round. I was facing towards the back doors, so I was in the perfect position to deliver a nice big portion of K9indness to these very deserving scoundrels. They didn't suspect a thing as they carried on their conversation.

'Did you see their faces?' Darren chuckled, tucking his greasy locks behind his ears. 'I thought they were going to pass out.'

'Haha yes, I think it was a bit of a shock,' said Barry, joining in with the laughter.

I was really angry to hear these horrible hoomans laugh about what they were doing. I moved into position and shuffled around until I was happy that this was the right spot. I was a bit concerned about the sheet and whether it was going to get in the way, but I needn't have worried.

As the van started, I used the engine noise to drown out my windy attack. As the F.A.R.T. system roared into action, I felt the K9indness hurtle towards the unsuspecting brothers.

WHOOSH!

As it did, the sheet lifted and flapped violently, like the huge sail of a boat in a storm.

I waited. Nothing. For a second, I thought it had failed, but then there was a cough and some choking from the front of the van.

'Aghh is that you?'Asked Barry, coughing as he spoke.

'No, it's you. Don't try to blame me,' said Darren, as he also struggled to clear his throat. This conversation continued back and forth for a few minutes as I settled back into my hiding place.

All of a sudden, there was silence, and I wondered what was going on. Then the older man spoke.

'Anyway bro, I think we've been here long enough now. We should get going.'

I thought he meant get going to the café and my heart sank, it hadn't worked.

But then he continued. 'I've been having a think, let me run this by you. Let's fix the roof now, we don't need any supplies. We can just put the felt back down, I have some sealant in the back of the van and it will be as good as new.'

Darren agreed enthusiastically. 'That's a great idea. It will only take half an hour and we can leave these nice people in peace.'

They opened the doors and began to get out.

'I'll just grab that sealant, it's here somewhere. 'Barry leaned over and began to rummage around in the back. I was sure I was going to be discovered when all of a sudden, his hand gripped something about six inches from my nose.

'Got it,' he said, and closed the van door.

I came out from underneath the sheet and thought it would be a good time to get out of the van. Luckily, the back doors opened easily as I pushed them with my nose. I jumped out and walked along behind the garden wall, making sure I kept out of sight.

I heard the men as they worked back up on the roof.

'That's all the felt damage sorted,' said Barry. They won't have any problem with that.

Darren climbed a little further up the roof near to the chimney. 'I just spotted there was some of the lead a little loose here,' he said. 'I've fixed it now. They may have got some water in there, if that hadn't been sorted.'

'Great work Daz,' said Barry, 'let's pack up, I think we're all done here.'

With that, they gathered their tools up and came down the ladder. At the bottom the couple were already waiting for them.

'That didn't take you long,' said the elderly man. 'Is everything OK?'

The two roofers looked at each other and smiled. It was Barry who spoke first.

'Yes, it's all done. We had everything we needed in the van so there was no need to get anything else,' he continued. 'We also found some damage near the chimney but that's fixed as well, so the roof is as good as new.'

The elderly lady looked across at her husband, and her concern was clear to see. 'Does that mean it will cost more?' she said. 'It's just that we…'

Before she had a chance to finish, Barry laughed loudly, making his belly shake, and replied. 'No, not at all. In fact, there is no charge. We had some materials in the van that were left over from another job and it really wasn't as bad as we first thought.'

'No charge?' said her husband. 'No charge? But… but we.'

Again, Barry interrupted. 'Look, it's the least we can do for such a lovely couple. If we can't help each other out, then it's a bit of a sad world, isn't it'?

His brother Darren agreed. 'Yes, it was only a small job. It didn't take long at all. We're glad we can help you out.'

As the words were coming out of the brothers' mouths, they looked surprised as they spoke. It was as if their ears couldn't understand all the nice things they were saying.

The couple thanked them over and over as they packed their tools away in the van. The two brothers said goodbye and drove off, leaving a very happy and relieved elderly couple, their belief in humanity restored.

A good job, I thought as I headed home. This superhero stuff was very rewarding. It was so nice to be able to help people, you get a really nice warm glow inside. It's nice to be nice.

I never really came across the Slater brothers again. I didn't need to. They carried on doing their roofing work in an honest way, and would always help hoomans who didn't have much money. They would fix leaks for free and they even did some gardening for local elderly residents to help them out.

They certainly had the K9indness, and I was proud that I'd been able to help.

CHAPTER 14
GROWLER

Growler went to the back door of the manor house, like he always did when he was called. As he waited to be summoned inside, he felt the uncomfortable shock collar around his neck. The collar was capable of delivering an electric shock to him, and was controlled by Lord Devlin or by one of his two nasty workers.

Things were all so different when he first arrived though. Everyone was really nice to him as he told them all about the workings of K9HQ, but soon afterwards it changed. They made him move out to the barn, and then the horrid shock collar was fitted. If he didn't do what he was told, they would use it and so now he had little choice but to obey them.

Growler was terribly depressed. He realised he'd done the wrong thing trusting this hooman. He had overheard them talking about K9HQ, and he knew his nasty master was very interested in getting his hands on something there, but he didn't know what it was.

For now, all he could do was follow his orders. Today his first job was to remind the hounds that they had foxes to chase. This meant being spiteful to them and getting them angry. He didn't like doing it, but what choice did he have?

Lord Devlin had seen his fortune getting smaller and smaller over the past few years. He enjoyed a lifestyle of fast cars and expensive holidays, but the upkeep on the manor was so much that before long he would run out of money. Fox hunting had been made illegal, but he still managed to get around that and run several hunts a year. This was getting harder though, as more people understood that his pretend trail hunts were really fox hunts and more of his income was being lost.

He needed to find something; something big, that would make him rich for life. This is where the dog and K9HQ came in. He had no time for Growler and only kept him because he was useful. In fact, the Lord didn't like any animals unless they could make him money.

He had grown up a lonely child. He was sent to boarding school when he was very young and it was pretty clear he wasn't really wanted at home. His parents never really showed him any love or affection, and the only time his father did anything with him was to go hunting and shooting. It was here that he developed a coldness towards living creatures and, in fact that coldness was now felt towards people as well. He never had anybody close to him growing up, and he now felt he didn't need anybody.

But he did need money. And fast.

He knew from Growler that K9HQ had developed the F.A.R.T. system which was used by their superhounds to deliver various potions and remedies to hoomans. It was all so sweet that these were all for the benefit of mankind, so sweet it made him feel nauseous. What a waste this was left with dogs to use when he knew he could make much better use of it.

In particular, he was very keen to get his hands on the STOPnSLEEP module that had been developed to help the

police dogs. He felt it was criminal that this wasn't being used more widely. He knew there would be many army generals and politicians around the world that would love to have this technology.

Imagine an army of dogs that could overpower opposing soldiers quickly and quietly. He got more and more excited when he thought about how much these countries would pay for it. It would make him rich beyond his wildest dreams and he would become the most powerful man on the planet overnight.

His only problem was how to get hold of it, and this is where the miserable dog he kept in the barn came in.

Lord Devlin was still imagining the life of riches this would bring him as he opened the back door to see Growler cowering on the doorstep.

'Down to the kennels with you!' he shouted menacingly. The big dog obeyed, not wanting the painful collar to be activated.

'Get those hounds ready for the hunt, we have a full day today.'

With that, he went back into the house still occupied by the thoughts of power and wealth.

CHAPTER 15
THE MIGHTY MONTALIERS

When I returned from my adventure with the two roofing brothers-turned-good, the others loved hearing the story. They did say, though, that they thought it was dangerous on my own.

'What if you'd got trapped in the van?' said Bailey, and I knew he had a point. It was no good being a superhero if I got myself into trouble.

'OK,' I agreed. 'From now on I'll make sure I let somebody know where I'm going.'

'We could be a little gang,' said Poppy. 'We could be your deputies, like assistant superhounds.'

The others all loved that idea, and so we agreed that it would make much more sense to be a team.

'The Mighty Montaliers!' said Cookie, and everyone laughed.

'I think that's great; we will be a very good team.' I said. 'Now, let's get started.'

Each week seemed to get busier as we came across hoomans who needed the K9indness.

On a walk one day, we heard lots of commotion from a local shop. Somebody had stolen a charity collection box and had made off with the contents. A little later as we continued towards the park, we saw a hooman sitting against a wall with the collection box in his lap. He was trying to open it and Dad told us to stay while he called the police.

The man was concentrating so much on the box that he never saw us as we approached, and when he did look up, all he saw was a group of dogs, so he just continued trying to open the box unconcerned. He didn't even stop what he was doing as I began to walk backwards towards him. When I got really close to him, he did finally glance up.

'What are you doing you stupid dog? Get away from me,' he said, and waved his arm in my direction.

I wasted no time in giving him a huge blast of K9indness with optimum tail waft.

WHOOSH!

So strong was the blast that the other dogs told me afterwards that they had seen his hair blow in the wind, and it looked as if it might blow it right off his head.

He let out a choked cry. 'Eww! What was that you disgusting animal?'

Those were the last nasty words that left his lips though, because it began to take effect. He got up with the collection box and headed back towards the shops. On his way he gave us all a stroke and even some chin scratches.

The thief returned to the shop and gave back the collection box. He apologised profusely, and no charges were brought by the police. From then on, every year, the man would collect money for the charity, and became one of their biggest fundraisers. He also developed a real love of dogs. I wonder why?

We saw and heard lots of conversations on our travels and one day I heard a man's voice and he was shouting very loudly. We were passing a restaurant and I could tell the voice was coming from there.

He was talking, or rather yelling, at a young hooman lady who was serving the tables.

'I've been waiting for TEN minutes for my order; this is not good enough!'

She looked upset as I peered through the window, and he continued.

'And you are useless! You got our drinks wrong, and now the food is late! Call yourself a waitress? Pah!'

This was enough to get her crying, and I knew I wanted to sort out this nasty man.

The problem was that dogs weren't allowed inside the restaurant, so this would need some figuring out. I told the others that they needed to create a diversion, and Cookie immediately had an idea. Before I could say another word, she ran into the restaurant and grabbed a bread roll from one of the tables.

This caused absolute chaos as all the staff began to try to grab her. Cookie easily evaded them, obviously enjoying the game. She ran round and round the tables, stopping just long enough for them to nearly catch up, before zooming off again.

This was the chance that I needed, and I slipped quietly into the restaurant, well as much as a hooge hairy dog as tall as the tables could slip quietly anywhere. I made my way over to the man, who was now shouting at his partner while his children looked on, clearly upset.

'You didn't back me up!' he shouted at her.

'Well dear, I think you may be over reacting: it's not that girl's fault, and you're upsetting her.'

That just made him worse, but I was now at the table and it was time to deliver. As I took aim, I glanced back to see the table cloth lift briefly as the K9indness headed his way.

WHOOSH!

This was Cookie's signal to leave, and she dropped the soggy slime covered bread roll and departed through the front door. The staff, just relieved to see her leave, started to tidy up the fallen chairs and scattered napkins that littered the floor. I took this opportunity to quickly slip out of the open back door.

The young girl sheepishly returned to the family, still waiting for their order, but what greeted her was a surprise to say the least.

The man was smiling, and he spoke quietly to her.

'I'm really sorry about my behaviour earlier,' he said, as she stood open-mouthed. He continued, 'there was absolutely no excuse for it, and I only hope you can forgive my awful attitude.'

She nodded, not saying a word and hardly believing what she was hearing.

For the rest of the meal, the man was a perfect customer, polite and quietly-spoken. To round off a very strange evening for the young waitress, he left her a very large tip. I am pretty sure he never spoke to anybody like that again and became a really good example of a kind hooman.

One of the funniest little escapades we had, was one day, when we were waiting outside the supermarket. Outside in the car park, two hooman ladies were having a mahoosive argument. They had both tried to park in the same spot and now neither would back down.

The car park was totally blocked as their cars stuck out on both ends of the space. They were so distracted by the argument that neither of them noticed me as I walked slowly up to them. Nor did they notice when I delivered a double blast of K9indness directly at them.

WHOOSH!

The only way you would notice anything had happened was when they both paused in the back-and-forth shouting match to give a little cough. After that the argument continued, but now it was both ladies wanting to give the space to the other. This went on for a few minutes before they just both burst out laughing and warmly hugged each other.

Two more hoomans who came to see that being nice is the best feeling ever. We left as they both parked up in different spaces and the car park went back to normal.

Sometimes though, something would go on that needed urgent action and a little more planning and this was the case with our next little adventure.

CHAPTER 16
MOHAMMED AND NAHAL

One of Molly's friends at the park had heard about what we were doing and came to her one day to tell her about something he'd seen. Next door to where he lived, there was a family who had recently arrived in the country from Afghanistan. This is a place a long, long way away, and it has lots of problems and wars.

Since they arrived, there had been nasty words written on the walls of their house. There had also been some name calling, and the night before a rock had been thrown at one of the windows and had broken it.

Mohammed and Nahal Sakhi had only arrived in the UK two months before. They had left their home and everything they had because of the awful things that were going on. Mohammed was a vetandhairyman in Afghanistan and his wife, Nahal, was a veterinary nurse. They cared mainly for the stray dogs and cats in their country and worked for a charity that tried to rehome them.

Their two children, Esin and Ashtak, were both at school. Since the new war had started though, Esin would have been forced to stay at home because girls were not allowed to have an education. The same would have happened to her mum, who would have had to give up work.

There were lots of other horrible things happening too, so the family decided to leave the country and start a new life in England. They had found a house, and the children were going to school and making new friends.

Mohammed and Nahal had both started new jobs in the work that they loved; helping an animal charity, and they were happy in their new lives... until the attacks started.

At first it was a few bits of rubbish thrown into the garden, but soon things began to get written on the walls. They weren't nice words, and Mohammed now checked every morning before the children came out so he could clean it off before they could read the hurtful messages.

All of their neighbours were really nice and were shocked at what was happening, but nobody wanted to get involved and there was a good reason for that. The latest incident was the worst one so far, and it had scared the whole family.

The police had attended, but they said without any sort of evidence it was difficult for them to do anything. It was then that Dinky, the Patterdale Terrier who lived with the family next door, decided to speak to Molly.

He had heard of some of the things that had happened to these nice hoomans and that there was a new superhero living close by. Word of Mighty Monty quickly spread around the dog world by Pee mail, and so Dinky knew exactly who to speak to.

Molly gathered us all round that evening and told us the story of what was happening to the poor family. We all agreed that we needed to do something so Bailey and Poppy said they would hang around outside to see who was doing these horrible things.

Cookie said it may be a good idea to do shifts as it could be any time of the night that the hoomans were coming round and causing the damage. We all agreed, and we worked it out so that somebody would be there all night and the others would cover back at home in case the hoomans noticed.

It was three nights later that Bailey came back out of breath and panting. He had seen two hoomans in dark clothes and hoods sneak up to the house. They were just about to throw something and so he barked... and kept barking. It alerted people in the houses and the two hoomans panicked and ran off. As they left, and in their anger, they threw the thing they had been holding, which turned out to be a rock, at Bailey. It had hit him on the leg and cut him, but he had managed to run all the way home to let us know. Poppy licked the wound clean for him and he assured us he was fine. He just really wanted us to get those nasty hoomans.

We needed to keep up our patrols because we had to find out who these people were. We agreed we should double up to be safe, and I said that when they were spotted, we needed to follow them back to their house. I wanted to know where these hoomans lived. I had an idea.

It was another couple of nights before they were spotted again, and this time they managed to throw a brick. Luckily it missed the window, but the two vandals ran and it was Cookie and Molly that followed them. They were like two secret agents as they trailed the nasty hoomans back to where they lived.

Every so often, they would stop and make sure nobody

was watching them and the two detective dogs would duck into a doorway or hide behind a car. This was a lot easier for Molly than Cookie, who was literally about ten times bigger.

Once the only place that she could hide was behind a lamp post, which was ridiculous considering her size. If they had looked properly, they would have seen her clearly sticking out from each side of the thin upright lamp. At one end a hooge panting tongue, while at the other her massive hairy tail would have been very visible...Especially as she was lying right under a light.

Luckily, our two criminals weren't too clever, and they were easily outsmarted by our daring duo. Eventually, after a few more games of hide-and-seek, the hoomans arrived back at their house and Molly and Cookie were able to report back to us. Now it was time for a new plan to be drawn up.

CHAPTER 17
TIME FOR A HOME VISIT

While we all agreed these two hoomans need a good burst of K9indness, I thought we needed to go a bit further. Maybe it wasn't just these two that were nasty, maybe they came from a family that had made them that way. If that was the case, I needed to try and get them all in one go. That is where things might get a little tricky.

We needed a good plan, but first I wanted to see if I could check out the family a little more. It didn't take very long to find out all about them. We took it in turns to watch the house and then report back. It was pretty easy because sometimes they went out into the garden. They seemed to enjoy loud music, drinking the water that made them fall over, and harassing their neighbours.

There were six of them, the two parents and four mini-hoomans, though two of these mini-hoomans were actually grown-up ones. These were the two that were causing the trouble at the house, but it soon became clear they all behaved in the same way.

This is what I wanted to see, because I knew that like dogs, mini-hoomans are not born nasty, but they can become that way if they are taught to; it's all down to the way that they are brought up. I thought it would be a waste to just zap those two older mini-hoomans and leave the rest. So that was it. I was going to have to give the whole family the K9indness.

We all spoke about how we could manage this, but eventually I just spoke up. 'There's only one way to do it as far as I can see.' They all listened as I continued. 'I'm going to just go into the house and get them all. It will just be a case of me giving all of them the K9indness before they get me.'

'It's a bit risky,' said Bailey.

'I know,' I agreed. 'The trouble is we've been going over this and I can't see any other way of doing it, can you?'

They all shook their heads and deep down we all knew this was the only way.

My plan was a simple one. If they were in the garden, I may be able to get them all in one go, but if not, I would need to get into the house. We waited and watched for a few days, but there was no sign of them all out in the garden together.

As well as this, the Sakhi's house had been damaged again. I decided it was time to act, I was going into that house.

I decided first thing in the morning would be the best time to try, as there would be more chance of everyone being there. I went around into the back garden and managed to squeeze between two broken fence panels. Once inside, I immediately saw their dog. He spotted me and came towards me, barking a warning. He was a very thin and neglected looking Staffordshire Bull terrier, and he was chained to a small wooden kennel.

I spoke to him as he approached. 'Take it easy brother, I'm here to help.' I didn't have time to explain everything, but I just said, 'Trust me and keep barking.'

He did as I asked and that had the effect I'd hoped for as suddenly the back door opened. This was my chance. As one of the mini- hoomans began to yell at the dog, I burst past her and into the kitchen of the house. What happened next can best be described as mayhem. As I got into the kitchen, the girl was screaming and yelling and turned to chase after me. This was my chance, and I stopped dead and delivered my first batch of K9indness.

WHOOSH!

It flew towards her and I just hoped it was a direct hit. I had no time to check because I had to keep moving.

The screaming girl had alerted the whole house, and there seemed to be hoomans everywhere. Next was one of the older mini-hoomans who had been attacking the house. He was right behind me, and reached out to grab my tail.

Bombs away!

The force of my delivery and the added tail swoosh, was enough to knock him off balance, and he ran straight into his brother and they both ended up on the floor.

'Get out, you mangey mutt!' he yelled at the top of his voice, but I just took a step backwards and delivered number three K9indness straight into his face as he sat on the floor. They both got to their feet coughing, and joined the girl in chasing me round the living room. I just had to hope it started working before they got me.

I still had three to go, and I need to go upstairs because there were no more hoomans in sight. As I ran up the stairs, the three were still in pursuit and closing in as I struggled on the steps with my hooge paws. I headed into the first room I saw and it turned out to be the bedroom of the remaining mini-hooman.

She was asleep in the bed and I decided the best approach was a direct one, so I leapt up next to her. I think it was fair to say she was surprised, and she sat up and let out a massive scream. Brilliant! That's perfect! I thought, as I spun around and gave her a burst of the good stuff.

WHOOSH!

Four down, two to go. So far so good, I thought.

The bad news was that I was now in a small room with four hoomans, and it looked like I was trapped. Four then became five as their dad's large body suddenly filled the doorway. My only option became clear, and I charged full speed at the hoomans. There are not many people that can handle being charged at full speed by a fully-grown, one hundred- and sixty-pound Newfydoof, and these hoomans were no exceptions.

I ploughed right through them and left them spinning and falling like a set of two-legged skittles. They were yelling and screaming, and trying to scramble to their feet. As I reached the door, their father stood between me and the exit. He tried to grab me but I sidestepped him, and it's fair to say he wasn't the most athletic hooman I've ever seen. I left him desperately grabbing at thin air, before he crashed down onto the carpet.

This had the effect of knocking over the chasing mini-hoomans for a second time and gave me the chance to blast dad.

WHOOSH!

Five down, one to go.

There was only one room left, and I hit the bathroom door like a Newfydoof wrecking ball. As I entered, the final hooman in my mission appeared. It was the mother, and she leapt out of the shower with the biggest scream I've ever heard. Now I have to say that if I was capable of blushing, I would have done because she had not had the opportunity to get dressed.

All of a sudden, she appeared to faint. I don't know whether that was seeing a mahoosive dog bursting into her bathroom and hurtling towards her, or the fact that she was now standing naked in front of the whole family who had followed me in. As she hit the floor, I backed up and delivered my final portion of K9indness.

WHOOSH!

Surely now though I was trapped, as all six hoomans and I were inside the small bathroom and the exit was very blocked.

But then the first girl that I had zapped when I came into the house ran over to her fallen mother. 'Are you OK Mum?' she said, with real concern in her voice.

One by one they went over to her. They covered her with a towel and helped revive her. I could hear all of them as I quickly headed down the stairs. They were being kind.

The Sakhi's had no more problems with their house or the family. In fact, one morning Mohammed came out to find that the whole front had been scrubbed, and the garden tidied. The whole neighbourhood was a quieter much nicer place to live. The family that I'd visited changed, and became kind and thoughtful neighbours. I was very happy about that because I NEVER wanted to visit their house again.

Bodger their long-suffering dog lived out the rest of his days in comfort with a comfy bed in front of the fire and plenty of treats.

When we all got back home, I told them what had happened in the house and everyone enjoyed the crazy chase story. It had been a good team effort, and we slept peacefully that night knowing we had successfully added some more K9indness to the world.

Chapter 18
A Warning

Things were pretty quiet for the next few days, until one of the assistants from K9HQ turned up in the back garden. Molly came in to tell me that they wanted to speak to me, so I followed her outside.

When we got into the garden, the small Cavalier King Charles Spaniel was pacing nervously backwards and forwards. 'Hi,' I said, 'is everything OK?'

'Not really, no,' she replied. 'We have a bit of a problem and DOG needs to see you urgently.'

'OK,' I said, 'but if there's trouble, I need the rest of the team to come as well.'

'That's not really the way it works,' she said. 'DOG usually only ever meets with the actual Superhero; not their support staff.'

'These aren't my support staff; they are my team and they need to come as well.' She was obviously flustered and in a hurry, so she agreed, and we all set off towards the woods.

On the way I told Cookie, Bailey and Poppy what to expect at K9HQ.

'Don't speak unless you're spoken to, be polite, and please don't call DOG a sausage dog.'

I looked at Bailey as I spoke. He had a habit of saying exactly what he was thinking before he engaged his brain. The last thing I wanted was to upset everyone, especially the boss.

When we got to the large oak tree, I could see the others looking around, confused. 'Follow me,' said the small dog impatiently. 'Through here.'

She squeezed into the passageway via the door that was beginning to open in the base of the tree.

I could see puzzled faces from Bailey, Poppy and Cookie, despite the fact they'd heard about the entrance before. We followed the assistant down the passage until we passed through the door at the end and into the now familiar white room.

'Wait here,' she said, 'I'll go and let them know you've arrived... all of you.' With that she left, closing the door behind her.

We didn't have to wait long before the door opened and DOG appeared flanked by the ever-present St Bernard and Dr Gold.

'I see we have new guests,' said DOG kindly. 'Welcome, I know how much you've been helping Monty, I'm glad you're here.'

'Please sit down and relax, everyone. We have some troubling news and it's possible you could be affected.' Everybody sat anxiously waiting to hear what DOG was about to say.

He waited until everyone had settled, then began to tell us the reason he'd brought us here.

We heard about the dog Growler and how he used to be a superhound. K9HQ had developed the power of talking to hoomans through mind messages, something that should have been used for good. Growler, however, had abused his power, and had given secrets to a bad hooman.

DOG spoke of how Growler was in the employment of Lord Devlin. We learnt that this hooman was a nasty man who would stop at nothing to get hold of the superpowers that K9HQ had developed and use them for his own financial gains.

DOG then explained that the F.A.R.T. system, and the STOPnSLEEP were the things he was desperate to have, and it was obviously imperative that this couldn't happen or else the world would become a dangerous place.

I let this all sink in for a minute and could see the others were also processing this pretty scary update.

'This all sounds awful,' I said. 'But if you don't mind me saying, how does this affect me? I only have the K9indness and he doesn't sound the sort of hooman who'd want that superpower.'

DOG nodded as I spoke and then replied. 'Normally Monty I'd agree with you, but there has been a worrying development.' He looked at St Bernard and then invited him to continue.

'We have a network of pups that keep us informed of developments in the world out there.' He pointed with his paw in the general direction of the exit. 'They keep us updated with the hooman world and we had an urgent message just this morning from your area.'

'Go on,' I said. It intrigued me to know what this news could be.

The big dog spoke slowly and deliberately. 'Growler was spotted in your area, and he was in conversation with three Pomeranians belonging to a Miss Fothergill.'

I was confused. 'Why would he be talking to them?' I asked.

'Well, we believe that Growler had heard about the incident with this hooman, and believes that you have the STOPnSLEEP Monty.'

'This is a worrying development,' continued DOG, 'and something we thought you needed to be aware of.'

'Well, I appreciate the warning,' I said, 'but I don't have the STOPnSLEEP. It's been removed.' I looked across at Honey to confirm it.

She nodded, but before she could say anything DOG said, 'Yes, but he doesn't know that.' He spoke with concern and I understood the point he was making.

St Bernard continued. 'We have to assume that Growler has got the information about the incident from the Pomeranians. We must also assume that he now thinks you have the STOPnSLEEP and has reported that back to Devlin.'

'We tried to neutralise his superpower of communicating with the hoomans after he left, but we don't think we've been entirely successful doing it remotely,' said Dr Gold.

'From now on we have to believe that you are at risk Monty,' said DOG with assurance. 'I can only apologise as all of this comes from our error but we can't change that now. We have to look at the present situation.'

'Monty, we are going to fit you with a tracker,' said Dr Gold.

'Do you think we could ever lose him?' chuckled Bailey, 'have you seen the size of him?'

St Bernard gave him one of his stern looks, and Bailey went quiet, allowing the Doctor to continue.

'Obviously we know where you are most of the time Monty, but if anything untoward should happen, this will tell us exactly where you are at any given time.'

The tracker was a very small device that was easily put into my neck by a simple injection. By now I was starting to feel like I'd been wrestling with a porcupine I'd had so many needles.

Then a tiny receiver was inserted in Molly's collar, and the Doctor continued with her explanation. 'To activate the device, you just need to bark three times. Do you want to give it a try now?'

I followed her instructions and gave three big barks, which echoed around the small room. As soon as I'd finished Molly's collar began to beep really loud and fast.

'Excellent,' she said, 'now bark three times again.'

Once more I did as she'd asked and the collar fell silent.

'Perfect,' she continued. 'So, the tracker was activated by your barking and the noise you heard, was the transmitter on Molly's collar. It was loud and fast because she was pretty much standing next to you. If you were further away the sound would be slower and quieter. You will need to practice when you leave but you will soon pick it up, it's all about distance and direction.'

I hoped it was that easy because I've seen those four

when they see a squirrel. All common sense goes out of the window and at that point I couldn't imagine them finding their own paw in front of their muzzle.

'We'll give it a go,' I said, unconvinced.

'The collar switches off on three barks, so if you activate it accidentally when the Postman comes, that's all you need to do,' she continued. 'It should only be switched on and left on if you need help. We have a second transmitter here in the lab so we will also be alerted.'

'OK,' I said, 'I feel a lot more reassured now, knowing that I have this.'

I wasn't really being totally honest because I really didn't think I'd ever need it, and also that nothing bad was going to happen.

DOG wrapped everything up by addressing all of us. 'I really can't stress enough how seriously we are taking this. You need to be alert at all times because this hooman is a very serious threat; believe me, this is real.' He looked straight at me when he said the last bit of the sentence. Did he just read my mind? I guess he is DOG after all. Why should I be surprised?

We all assured him that we would take the news seriously, and he bid us farewell and good luck. As we left through the door from where we arrived, Dr Gold said, 'Remember Monty I'll know where you are at all times. I won't let you down.'

We smiled at each other as I turned and followed the others down the passageway.

Chapter 19
Hide and Seek

As we emerged back into the woods, there was lots of excited chatter. Cookie, Poppy and Bailey were all trying to take in everything they'd seen, while Molly and I discussed the tracker.

'We should give it a go,' said Molly, 'while we're here in the woods.'

Well, it would be a good time to practise. I thought, while it's fresh in everyone's mind.

'Yes,' said Bailey, 'you go and hide Monty – that should be fun. 'They all agreed, and I told them to give me about five minutes to get far enough away, and then follow the transmitter noise.

'You all need to close your eyes though, or you'll see what direction I'm heading in.'

'OK' said Bailey. 'We'll just ignore all the broken undergrowth and fallen trees...you know, the way we'd usually know which way you're heading.'

'Very funny,' I said. 'Just follow the tracker – OK?'

They all agreed, and closed their eyes as I headed as carefully as I could in the direction of the lake. As I got round to the other side, I saw the canal and a small bridge, and thought that would be a great place to test it out. I quietly went into the tunnel under the bridge, where I was out of sight.

Now settled, I did three big barks to set off the tracker and just as I finished the last one, I heard a big splash. As I turned around, I saw a hooman fisherman struggling to pull himself out of the water and back onto the bank.

I hadn't noticed him when I snuck into the darkness under the bridge and, as I barked, it startled him so much that he lost his balance and fell into the canal.

He was grumbling and muttering under his breath as he began to squeeze his trousers and jacket in an attempt to get rid of the excess water. I thought it may be best if I found another hiding place, and crossed the bridge to a small wood on the other side and hid behind a group of small trees.

Meanwhile, Molly and the others were trying to figure out how the transmitter worked. Once I'd activated the tracker, the collar began to beep steadily and fairly quietly. At first, they went in the wrong direction and the beeps got slower. They kept changing direction until the sounds speeded up. As they moved in my direction, the sound got a little louder as well.

They soon worked out that the louder and faster the beeps, the closer they were getting. A few times, they veered off the wrong way, and the transmitter slowed down. They soon got back on track and it appeared they were getting closer.

As they got to the canal, they saw the bridge and as they got closer, they saw a hooman looking nervously at them, clothes still dripping with water.

'Funny thing to go swimming in all your clothes,' said Poppy to the others. They all nodded in agreement as they looked at him on their way to the bridge.

'It's a hooman,' said Cookie. 'Have you ever been able to work them out?' Again, they all nodded, and crossed over the bridge, following the very loud and fast beeping coming from Molly's collar.

It was very soon afterwards that they found me, proving that the tracker and transmitter worked well. I still thought it was all a waste of time and that nothing was going to happen.

We crossed back over the bridge and past the soggy fisherman as we headed home. He was still grumbling and dripping wet and so we took a wide berth around him.

CHAPTER 20
DON'T DROP LITTER

As we made our way back through the woods, we spotted some hoomans on the path so we kept a low profile. We've startled people before when all of a sudden, the five of us come heading towards them out of the woods, so we took a path off to the side.

As we got level with them, we could see it was two hooman men followed by a lady and man walking together. They seemed to be having some sort of disagreement, so I listened in. The couple seemed unhappy about something and I could hear the lady saying they should pick up their rubbish.

It became clear that the men were throwing litter on the floor and as I watched, one of the men threw an empty can into the undergrowth. I was getting the conversation clear now and as he did it he turned round to the lady and shouted;

'Make me!' They both laughed.

The man who was walking with her tried to reason with them.

'There's a bin just up there lads, this is a lovely area that everyone likes to enjoy.' The other one turned round and looked at them both as he dropped an empty bag on the floor and they both laughed again.

The couple decided that things could turn confrontational and kept quiet as the smirking hooman men headed for

the woods exit. I decided to act, and began to run along
the path we were on. This path was parallel to the one the
hoomans were on, and my aim was to get in front of them
and to beat them to the exit.

I may not be too fast, but I was certainly capable of
beating a couple of unruly hoomans, and I quickly overtook
them. As I cut across towards the exit, I was now in front
and my plan was to 'get them' at the small footbridge that
led to the car park.

The others hung back as I put my plan into action and as
the hoomans came through the gate, I was standing there
blocking their progress across the bridge.

'Man, there's a cow blocking the bridge,' said one of the
men.

'Come on, Moo-ve out the way,' said the other, as they
both laughed. He then took a swing and kicked me on the
backside to get me to clear the bridge.

That was my signal and as his foot connected, I gave
them both a blast of K9nindness. Unfortunately, at that
very moment a hooge gust of wind blew, and I feared that
my delivery had blown off course. The two men jumped
past me and across to the other side of the stream. They
showed no sign of being any nicer, so I decided I needed to
think of another plan.

My last chance came as they got into their car. The
one closed his door while the other emptied his door
compartment of all of his rubbish onto the ground. It
looked like weeks of food wrappers and drinks cans, and he
did it just as the couple arrived into the car park.

I could see them looking with disgust as the litter blew across the car park.

'There's a bin just there,' the lady pointed out.

The man ignored her, and turned to close his door just as I rammed my rear end into the remaining gap. I now had an enclosed space, and I wasted no time in delivering a double blast. The two men began choking and spluttering as the K9indess tornado hit them.

WHOOSH!

They both jumped out of the car, still trying to clear their throats, but now the shock had turned to anger.

'What's wrong with you, you crazy dog?' said the man whose door I'd wedged with my bum. 'You're going to get it now!' With that, he began approaching me menacingly as the other one made his way behind me.

I wasn't sure how long the K9indness was going to take to work and before it did this could be a problem. I decided to give them both some warning barks as I retreated. As I did, I suddenly heard a loud and fast beeping coming from the bushes. The others had caught up, and I'd just set Molly's transmitter off with my barking.

The four of them emerged from the undergrowth where they'd been watching things unfold and immediately the men looked a little less confident. It wasn't just the fact that there were now five dogs in front of them, but that one of them was bleeping, and there was a red flashing light coming from its collar.

'Look!' said one of the men, pointing at Molly, 'That one's got a bomb – let's get out of here.'

They both began backing up towards their car, keeping us in sight and obviously ready to run if the exploding dog got any nearer.

We moved away now the threat was over, but I wanted to keep my eye on them. As they reached the car, I saw one of them look around the car park. Then he opened his door and reached inside. When he turned round, I saw he was holding a large bag. He walked slowly round the car and began to pick up the rubbish that was strewn across the tarmac.

He looked confused as he was doing it but when his friend joined him, it began to appear a lot more natural. He walked across to the bin, but just before he put the bag inside his friend called him.

'Hang on, there's some more in the woods. Let's pop back in and get that as well.'

His friend nodded, and they both crossed the small footbridge and went back into the woods. The couple who had been in the argument with them looked at each other, bemused. Then they looked at the men heading into the woods with the same confused expression on their faces.

Finally, they both turned to look at us. I barked three times to switch the frantic transmitter off and looked across at the others. 'Come on,' I said, 'let's go home.'

CHAPTER 21
INFORMATION IS POWER

Lord Devlin looked down at the nervous Akita that stood shaking in front of him. Growler had lost any trust he'd ever had in hoomans soon after he moved into the barn on the Lord's estate. He had been shocked with the collar, starved, and left with no warmth or comfort when it suited his evil master. He had learnt, painfully, that the only way he escaped punishment was to do exactly what he was told.

'So, what have you found out for me?' said the man menacingly. He stood over Growler purposely to be more intimidating, reminding him that he was very much in charge.

The dog had been sent to find out more information about a report of a dog who may be in possession of a superpower. It had been witnessed by three Pomeranians who lived with a hooman who had been allegedly attacked.

Growler was a large intimidating dog to look at, and Devlin knew that was usually all that was needed to get results. He had been sent with special instructions to find out what had happened, and to use any methods necessary to get the information the Lord required.

He knew that going back without the facts behind the story would mean real trouble for him. As it turned out, the Pomeranians were more than happy to talk about the incident. Growler was relieved because although his life had taken a few wrong turns recently, inside he was a good dog and wished them no harm.

Now he could go back to the manor house and give Lord Devlin the information he wanted. He had done what had been asked of him and so he would escape any punishment and maybe even get a little extra food that evening.

Now he retold the story back to the hooman using the limited mind transfer powers that he had left. When he left K9HQ disgraced and stripped of his superhero status, he realised they had been unable to completely erase his power of communicating with the hoomans. At first he was pleased, but he soon realised how it could be used for evil by the hoomans, and this is what had happened with Lord Devlin.

He never used the power anymore other than with the Lord, who knew about it and controlled the dog with the electric collar. If he could he would completely rid himself of his power, but for now, he was trapped.

As he heard Growler's account of the incident, the Lord became more and more animated. It seemed that the Pomeranians' hooman was rendered unconscious by a hooge dog who appeared to blow something at the lady from his rear end. This had to be it. This had to be the STOPnSLEEP delivered by F.A.R.T. He had finally found a dog who had this power and his excitement grew as a plan formed in his evil mind.

The dog was a Newfoundland called Mighty Monty, and the Pomeranians had also been able to tell Growler where the hooge dog lived.

'Good boy Growler,' said lord Devlin. Though he said the words, there was no warmth in his voice. Growler didn't care. Not being punished was enough for him. 'Extra food tonight for you. Now back to the barn, I don't need you again...FOR NOW.'

The last words were said with an inevitability that Growler's work was far from done.

As the large dog made his way out, he passed Bob Grimly and Stanley Gough as they came in through the back door. They were skulking humourless men and Growler tried to avoid them as much as he could. This wasn't always that easy considering the men also lived on the estate, but there was something about these hoomans that made the fur on his back stand up whenever he saw them.

They pushed past him as they came through the kitchen. Grimly muttered something unpleasant to him as they made their way into see Lord Devlin. As they closed the door behind them, something made Growler hang back. He wanted to hear what the men were talking about. He had a bad feeling about all of this, and he was right.

Though it was hard to hear everything clearly, he did manage to pick out most of the conversation between them.

'We need the stable ready today,' said the Lord with authority. 'I need you to make sure it's secure and there is nothing visible from the outside. We don't want any nosey passers-by to know about our visitor do we?'

'No Sir, we don't,' came the reply from Bob. 'We'll make sure it's all safe and sound, don't you worry about that Lord

Devlin.'

Grimly spoke next. 'When should we be expecting our guest sir?' The two men both laughed like evil villains from a Disney film.

'I want to go through it with you both later,' said Devlin. 'I have all of the details of where we can find them. I've instructed Dr Vengle to join us. I think he's going to be very important.'

Growler left as he heard the men heading back to the door. As he went back to the barn, he felt troubled.

This was not good.

Chapter 22
Lizzie Brown

Lizzie Brown kissed her grandma on her forehead as she picked up her tray. 'Bye Nan, I'm off to school now.'

The old lady smiled and gave a little wave as she settled down in her chair. 'Goodbye Lizzie, have a lovely day.'

Lizzie left and closed the door, leaving her grandma looking out of the window onto the garden. She put the dishes on the kitchen counter and went out through the back door into the small yard. She opened the shed door, and was immediately met with excited whooping coming from a large hutch in the corner. Lizzie greeted the two Guinea pigs, Blossom and Bluebell with affection, and filled up their food bowl. This silenced the two small rodents almost immediately, and Lizzie smiled as she topped up their water bottle.

Going back into the kitchen, Lizzie opened a tin of cat food that she took from the overhead cupboard. Suddenly, from nowhere, Luna appeared at her feet and began to rub herself against Lizzie's leg, purring loudly. Lizzie emptied the contents of the tin into a small bowl with the cat's name on it. As she placed it onto the floor, Luna began to pick eagerly at her fish smelling breakfast. Lizzie gave her a stroke and went into the lounge to get her coat and bag.

She shouted goodbye once more as she left the house, and closed the front door behind her and locked it. Her mum would be home from her night shift very soon, so her grandma wouldn't be alone for very long.

Lizzie's grandma had been struggling with her health for the past few years and so she moved in with Lizzie and her mother so they could look after her. Lizzie's mum worked nights at the hospital, so she helped out as much as she could around her schoolwork.

As she left the house and headed towards the high school, she began to get the familiar nervous feeling she had every morning. It was as if her stomach was churning around and nothing she could do would make it stop. It wasn't school. Lizzie enjoyed her lessons and liked her teachers. She just didn't really fit in. Growing up Lizzie had never found making friends very easy. She felt different to most of the other children she knew, and most of the time preferred to spend time at home with Luna and her two Guinea pigs, Blossom and Bluebell.

She loved reading and would immerse herself in stories that took her to exotic lands with fantastic characters. Nearly everyone else at school spent most of their time on their phones and it seemed her not having one made her stand out as different to almost everyone else.

It wasn't easy going out, even if she felt she wanted to. Her grandma needed to be looked after and Lizzie's mum was on her own providing for them, so she needed to help out. At home, she wasn't unhappy. She was very close to her mum and grandma and loved spending time with her pets. She felt truly happy when she could spend time around them.

The school day however, made her feel anxious. She

knew what to expect and things had been getting worse recently. Some of the other girls at school had begun to be mean to her. It had started with a few comments aimed in her direction about her appearance. She had red hair, and this seemed to be a target for many of the comments. At first, she just tried to ignore it but recently things had got worse and going to school made her worried about what the day would bring. The name calling picked on everything about her appearance, not simply her hair. Added to that, the fact that her lifestyle was different started to attract some really nasty and cruel comments.

In the past week, two incidents had happened that took things to the next level. She had been pushed, and had her hair pulled. The nastiness aimed towards her was escalating into physical harm, and as she walked to school, her anxiety began to increase.

CHAPTER 23
BULLIES

We had been out for a walk in the morning but mid-afternoon Dad suddenly announced we should go out again. 'It's a lovely day. We should make the most of it,' he said.

Not everyone was that keen, but Cookie and I decided to go. First, we could make sure Dad kept out of trouble and second, because it would be an hour away from the spangles and we'd be able to get some peace. We went out through the woods and down to the canal where we followed the path to the bridge where I'd helped the hooman go swimming. After that we walked up by the high school and as we went past the midi-hoomans were just on their way home.

We had the usual passing comments...

'Look you could put a saddle on them!'

'They're not dogs, they're horses!'

'Look – It's a pandacow!'

'I wonder how big their poos are?'

'I could ride those into battle...'

I remember a time when some of these were quite funny. Actually, I can't, but I'm sure when hoomans say them they sound funny in their own heads.

Anyway, we were getting the usual comments and laughter, but as we walked along, I noticed a group of three girls following closely behind one who was on her own. They were laughing, but it seemed like it was more at her and not with her. There was just something about them that looked odd.

Now the great thing about being a superhero is that you get to use your powers, and it was very easy for me to listen in even though they were a distance from us. What I heard wasn't very nice. They were obviously saying things about the girl. They were calling her nasty names and being very spiteful. They were laughing about her and I could hear her quietly sobbing.

It was at this point that we turned off the road and headed towards home. There was nothing I could do, and I looked across at Cookie, but I don't think she'd noticed. With so many hoomans around, she was having fun seeing how much slobber she could leave on the school uniform of anyone that got within her range.

When we got back, we had dinner and once the hoomans were in the other room looking at the telly box, I gathered everyone around.

I explained what I saw outside the school and how the three girls seemed to be being nasty to the one on her own. They were shocked when I told them what I'd seen and heard.

'Why do the hoomans behave like this?' Molly said sadly. 'It seems such a waste of time being nasty when you could just be happy.' The others all agreed.

'I don't know,' I replied, 'I have never been able to work out the hoomans. They are very complicated. I do know that I have a job to do now. I can spread the K9indness, and I think this needs to be next on the list.'

Again, they all nodded in agreement. 'Yes definitely,' said Bailey, 'We just need a plan.'

Molly had an idea. 'How about tomorrow at the same time we all go to where you spotted them?' She looked over at me as she spoke. 'We could all see them, and maybe get an idea of the best way of introducing them to Monty's Fast Air Response Tool.' We all laughed at Molly's idea but agreed it would be the best next step.

'OK,' I said, that's the plan sorted. Let's do this.'

The next day we all pretended we were sleeping when Dad wanted to go for an afternoon walk. In the end, he went out with Mum and it was our opportunity to sneak out of the back door and across the fields. We took the path through the woods that comes out by the high school and then we spread out and waited.

Sure enough, before long I spotted the girl again. Almost straight away, the same three girls were behind her. Yesterday's events were repeated, and I could hear the laughing and nasty comments. This time we were able to follow for longer and we stayed behind them until we got to the path through the woods.

This was obviously the place where the three girls took a different route home. Before they turned off, one of them threw a half-eaten sandwich at the girl on her own. It hit her on her back, and the three all laughed out loud and pointed their phones at her to film her trying to pick bits of tuna and mayonnaise out of her hair.

She just continued on her way, trying to ignore what was happening, and the girls seemed to lose interest and took the path into the woods. We followed them, but not before Molly demonstrated her superpower, and cleaned up the discarded sandwich that was scattered across the pavement.

The woods were pretty quiet, with just a few school children and the occasional dog walker. It soon became clear this trio of bullies weren't content with just picking on this girl. They made comments to pretty well everyone that walked past and at one point, one of them threw a stick at a little dog that had approached them, tail wagging, to say hello.

They needed the K9indness for sure, and it seemed we had found the perfect place to deliver it. Now we just needed to go home and come up with a strategy.

That night when she got home, Lizzie spoke to her mum about what was happening at school. She hadn't wanted to because she felt her mum had so much more to worry about, but she also knew she'd understand. She had always said to her, 'Whatever happens you can always talk to me, I'm always here for you.'

'Don't worry Lizzie,' Mum said, 'you did the right thing talking to me about it. We'll get this sorted love; I'll speak to the school tomorrow. I know they take bullying very seriously.'

CHAPTER 24
THE PERFECT PLAN... OR IS IT?

Now I don't like to brag but I have to say if there was ever a 'National Great Plan Day' my idea to make the bullies a little more compassionate would get hash-tagged for sure.

As we discussed our next mission that evening, we all agreed that the woods would make the perfect place to carry out the K9indness delivery. It was at that point that I had my great idea. Of course, we had a secret weapon; Cookie.

In terms of adding an element of surprise to somebody's day, she is an expert. I have seen her many times after a run in the woods emerging from the trees. She is coated in so much undergrowth she looks like a hooge hairy tree with legs. The slobber is nearly reaching the floor in two elastic shoelaces. And her tongue has grown to the length of a small python.

I explained to the others what I was thinking.

'If this is to work, we need to be well organised.' They all nodded. 'Along the route we need lookouts so we can coordinate the attack. Molly, Poppy and Bailey, this will be your job. As they pass your position, you give one bark to let the next lookout know, OK?'

They were OK with that and understood what they had to do. I continued. 'On the third bark, Cookie will begin her charge through the woods. You need to collect as many bits of branches, brambles and leaves on your coat as possible.'

'Just like a normal walk for Cookie then?' laughed Bailey.

'I guess so,' I said. He was right. I didn't really need to tell her. This was normal Cookie.

'OK Cookie, just run through the woods like you always do and come out on the path right behind the three targets.'

'What then?' she asked.

'Well, this is the best bit Cookie,' I continued as the others sat transfixed. 'You just scare the living daylights out of them.'

'I can do that,' she said eagerly.

'I know Cookie, I know.'

I went on to explain that this was the crucial bit, and Cookie needed to get the three not-so-kind hoomans running, hopefully terrified, down the narrow path. Hopefully that would mean they wouldn't be concentrating and would only see me at the last minute as I blocked their escape route.

The next day, we set out well before the end of the school day. I wanted us all in position before everyone came out and started to walk home. We would be ready and waiting in plenty of time.

Molly took the first position just off the path. About five minutes further down, Bailey got into his spot. At the same distance, Poppy was the last member of our lookout team and she got ready just out of sight.
Cookie went deep into the woods and began her task

of undergrowth and branch collecting – or just running around.

I then went down to where I was going to lay in wait. It was a section of the path with a small bridge that crossed a shallow, muddy stream. The path got narrow at this point so it would be perfect to trap our unsuspecting bullies.

Then it was all about waiting. The planning had gone well. It was perfect. In fact, it was genius. Fool proof even.

The only problem was I hadn't foreseen the unpredictable element...

The spangles.

CHAPTER 25
IF YOU GO DOWN TO THE WOODS

Before long, we could hear the excited voices of schoolchildren leaving for the day. It was a large school, so home time was always busy.

This was our signal to get prepared, and I lay down just off the path and waited.

The three girls appeared about ten minutes later and walked down the path on their familiar route home. As they passed Molly's position, she stepped out, barked once and then made herself scarce again. The girls looked round briefly but didn't spot her and continued along the path.

Next, they reached Bailey's position and once again, as they went past, the signal was repeated. The three girls heard the bark again but weren't alarmed as there was nothing in sight.

That was two, so I readied myself, as the third one would signal Cookie's charge through the woods. The plan was going well. Or so it seemed.

Poppy though had been waiting in her spot for a little too long, and had got bored. She had also caught the scent of some fox poo and the temptation to wander off and roll in it proved too much for her. This meant when the girls reached the point where she should have been, there was no lookout and the plan was in serious danger of collapsing.

I was beginning to think something had gone wrong, but I mistakenly assumed that maybe the three girls had stopped along the path for some reason. In fact, they were well past Poppy's position when she wandered back, oblivious of her failure as a lookout. She glanced up the path, but no sign of them yet. But as she turned around, she just caught a glimpse of them as they disappeared around the corner.

She quickly barked, hoping that things would still work as planned. Cookie and I heard the final signal, and I got myself ready for her charge and hopefully some fleeing hoomans. She had done a great job with her undergrowth collection and as she bounded through the woods, her fur was hardly visible under the cover of brambles, branches and nettles.

The only problem was that she was too late. The delay in Poppy's bark had meant that the girls had gone well past the point that she came out of the woods onto the path. As she burst through the bushes, there was no sign of them. Maybe she was too early. She was confused and so she ran a little way back up the path, carefully looking, so as not to give her presence away.

No sign of them, though. She started to panic. Where were they? She went a little further, but once she reached Poppy she realised she'd missed them.

They must have got past her somehow, and that's when Poppy owned up.

'I may have been a bit late with my bark...'

'What do you mean?' said Cookie. 'Late?'

'Well, I got a little distracted...'

It was at this point that the pungent smell of 'Eau De Fox Poo 'sneaked into Cookie's nostrils. Suddenly it was clear and she shook her head. 'Oh Poppy, you've messed it up. They will be reaching Monty and he's got no back up. Come on we need to get there, fast!'

They began to race down the path in the hope that the operation could still be saved. As they got round the corner, they came face to face with an elderly couple out for an afternoon stroll with their Poodle, Oscar.

What confronted them was a hooge bear-like creature covered in branches and bits of bramble. It was running straight towards them, its massive tongue flopping around in the air and drool almost reaching the floor. They quickly jumped to the side as the creature ran past, but poor Oscar was too slow.

As Cookie and Poppy passed and the dust settled on the path, the couple looked down at the poor little dog, who had been covered almost head to tail with slobber.

He stood with strings of slimy goo dripping down, and his coat was covered in leaves and twigs. They all stood there in shock for a while, before continuing their walk in the hope that the rest of it would be more peaceful.

In my position near the bridge, I suddenly spotted the three girls. They were casually strolling along, laughing and looking at their phones. Where was Cookie? She should be right behind them. How was I going to get this to work?

CHAPTER 26
PLAN B

I needed to buy some time, so I stood in the middle of the path and let out a loud deep bark. This seemed to work, and the three mean girls suddenly stopped as they were confronted by a massive black and white dog in the middle of the path. I just stood my ground, hoping that I would look scary enough to hold them up.

Obviously, they decided I wasn't, and they continued coming towards me, shouting the usual horse and cow comments and laughing at their own wittiness.

Just as they reached the bridge, I heard loud paw-steps from behind them. It could mean only one thing and sure enough, Cookie appeared a second later followed by Poppy trailing in her wake. They were sprinting at an unstoppable pace and were heading straight towards the three giggling hoomans.

As they turned to face the on-rushing bramble monster, squeals and screams filled the air. Phones and school bags went flying, as the girls dropped everything in their panic. What was approaching them at speed was such a shock that at this point, our plan took an unexpected twist.

Instead of running towards me where I would dispatch three helpings of K9indness, our victims took a different route. All three in unison, jumped over the side of the bridge and into the stream below. The drop was only a few feet, and the water was shallow, but wow, that mud was deep. It was also very smelly.

As we peered over the bridge, we saw the girls knee deep in squelchy, slimy, stinky mud. They were all slowly slurping their way towards the bank, their shoes stolen by the black tar-like sludge.

This was my chance. I quickly ran round to the bank and began to reverse towards them as they attempted to get themselves out.

'What is that thing doing?' shrieked one of the girls, as I got closer to them. 'Get away! I'm calling the dog warden!'

Well, I knew that wasn't the case, especially as I could see her phone and it was currently under one of Cookie's hooge paws on the path.

I let out three blasts in quick succession...

WHOOSH!

My tail swished the K9indness directly into the three angry and muddy faces of the girls as they neared the bank.

WHOOSH!

I let out three more just in case and again it was directed straight towards them.

WHOOSH!

Now the coughing, spluttering and gagging could be heard, as the delivery hit its target. I was used to this now, and it was a wonderful sound. I knew that within minutes, it would begin to work.

We retreated back up the path and kept a watch to make sure they escaped from the mud safely. They did, and they even managed to find a few of their shoes. Even from this distance, we could see a change. Smiles instead of frowns and much kinder words could clearly be heard as they helped each other from the stream.

'Come on,' I said, 'let's go and find Molly and Bailey. It's time to go home. Mission complete.'

Lizzie never had a problem with those girls again. The school had already sorted the problem out before our intervention, but at least nobody else would become their victim. In fact, they all became friends, and they regularly visited Lizzie's house and enjoyed playing with Blossom and Bluebell.

We went home and spent the evening chuckling at the day's events. We settled down to a well-earned sleep, unaware of the events that would unfold over the coming days, and the sinister plot being hatched at Lord Devlin's manor house.

CHAPTER 27
DOCTOR VENGLE

Dr Harold Vengle was a horrible hooman. There was no other way of describing him. He was;

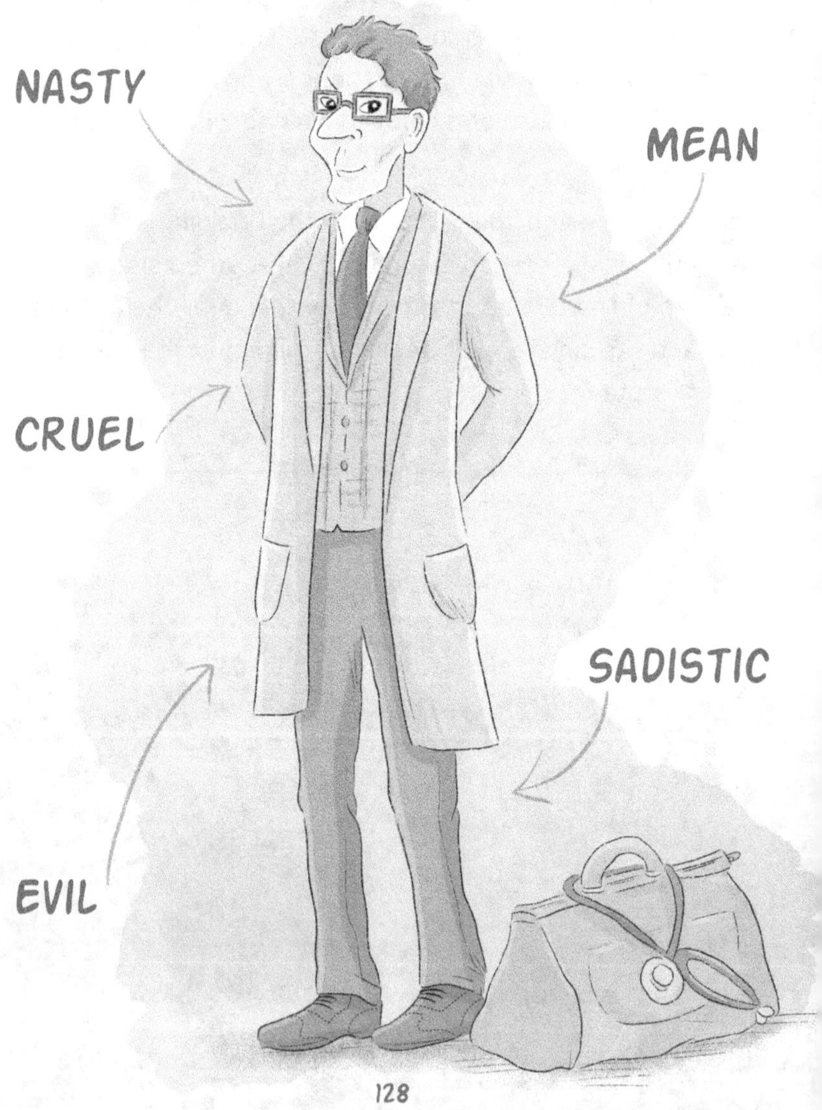

So, it turns out there were other ways of describing him, though none of them made him any nicer.

He was a vetandhairyman and had taken an oath to help and protect animals. That oath though, had been forgotten about many years ago. The only thing that Dr Vengle was interested in was helping himself, and he would do anything for money. When nasty hoomans wanted something illegal or just plain wrong, they would come to him. Everyone knew he would do whatever you wanted... as long as you had enough cash.

This is how he first came to the attention of Lord Devlin. The two men got along really well, as both had the same darkness inside them. Neither seemed capable of kindness or compassion, and now they were united in planning a truly heinous act.

The Doctor was a tall and spindly man. He had a look of self-importance about him. He was always smart, with an immaculate tweed suit and waistcoat underneath his expensive Saville Row raincoat.

He always wore Italian brogues so highly polished that you could see your face in them. He drove a jet-black Range Rover that gleamed almost as brightly as his shoes.

Yes, Dr Vengle certainly liked the finer things in life, but that was OK, he had plenty of money. He had discovered many years ago that there were hoomans who would pay him handsomely for his lack of morality and his willingness to keep things under wraps.

It was this greed that brought him here today to Lord Devlin's manor house. To be more precise, it was to the stable block close to the house. The wooden stables had been constructed after the house but had an old and neglected feel to them. Like all of Lord Devlin's accommodation for his animals, it was basic and lacked any type of comfort. There were six individual stables and Dr Vengle stood inside an empty one at the end of the row.

He was not alone. He was joined by Lord Devlin and his two mean workers, Bob Grimly and Stanley Gough. In the corner sat the nervous figure of Growler. who had been brought from his barn by the two men. He was clearly uncomfortable about the situation he found himself in.

Harold Vengle had with him his medical bag. The ageing brown leather bag contained everything he would need for what they had planned. He unclipped the brass clasp and opened the bag. Placing it on a small table in the stable, he began to remove the contents.

As he placed the shiny metal instruments onto the table, even the other men looked uncomfortable. When he'd finished, he stood back from the table. 'There,' he said with satisfaction. 'That will do nicely. When are we expecting our guest?'

Lord Devlin stepped in front of his two assistants and spoke to the vet. 'Now we have this in place, we are ready. The stable has been made secure, as you can see.'

The men all looked around the stable as if to check that it was indeed as he had said. The barred window had been covered by dark plastic and the stable door had two large bolts on the outside. In the corner of the stable there was a large dog crate. Bob Grimly spoke as the men looked at it.

'It's the biggest one they did sir.' He looked at his employer for approval.

Lord Devlin nodded, and an unpleasant grin spread across his face. 'Well, it doesn't matter if it can move or not, does it? Besides, it won't be in it for too long.'

The men laughed nervously, as if that's what they thought they should do.

'We do have one potential problem though,' he continued. 'Once we have our guest with us, is there any chance he can be found?'

'We'll be very careful, sir,' replied Stanley Gough. 'Once we have the dog in our possession, we'll make absolutely certain we aren't followed.'

Both men nodded and looked back at their boss for approval.

'I am more concerned about any type of monitoring or tracking devices they might have over at K9HQ,' he replied. 'We are talking about their prized possessions, their pretend super heroes. They may take precautions. I don't want to take any risks that this operation could fail and that's why I've invited our friend to join us.'

He looked across at Growler, who hadn't moved from the spot he was in when everyone arrived. 'As an ex-employee of K9HQ, I know that Growler here will have some very valuable insights into the type of security arrangements they have, isn't that right Growler?'

The dog looked back anxiously at the man as he finished talking. He didn't want to be any part of what was happening. He knew what they had planned, and he felt disgusted by it. But he was trapped.

He tried to be vague as he sent his thoughts back to Lord Devlin. He knew that they had developed trackers, but he felt if he could stop them finding this out, their plan might fail.

Lord Devlin wasn't accepting his lack of cooperation, and he looked across at Bob Grimly and nodded. 'Maybe this will help you remember,' he said, as the man held the all too familiar device so that the dog could clearly see it. Devlin nodded again and the man pressed the button on the device.

Growler yelped and jumped back in pain as the electric collar around his neck was activated. It zapped him with a painful blast of volts.

'Now,' said Devlin, 'let me ask you again, and this time try a little harder to remember.' He spoke and sneered menacingly, and the cowering dog knew he was in an awful situation.

This time, he relayed the information that Lord Devlin wanted to know and the man smiled triumphantly. 'There, that wasn't too hard, was it? Take him back to the barn.' As he barked his instructions, he waved at Grimly and Gough. 'Then get back here... We have plans to make.'

CHAPTER 28
A REQUEST

I had been pretty busy since the school incident. K9indness seemed to be in big demand. I had sent windy goodness to a pushy door-to-door salesman, and a hooman man shouting at a lady with a guide dog. On top of that, I had converted a would-be burglar into a member of the local neighbourhood watch, and recruited two youths who threw water at a homeless man as volunteers at their local food bank.

It was tiring though, all this superhero stuff. There was more need for the K9indness than I ever thought. Usually, I just used the power when I saw things as we were out and about, but sometimes, I'd get requests and that was what happened on THAT day.

I was pottering around in the garden when I heard someone calling my name. Now, with my super hearing, this could be close or from a distance, so I tried to get a fix on where it was coming from.

Then I heard it again.

'Monty, it's me, Lucy.' Lucy was a German Shepherd who lived about six doors down. Now that she spoke again, I knew where to look and I could see her head above the fence.

'I've just heard a man shouting at his dog over in the woods at the back, and I'm sure he was hitting it. I thought you'd want to know.'

I did. I hadn't heard anything, but maybe it was before I came out into the garden.

'Thanks,' I replied, 'I'll have a look.'

The others were all in the house snoozing, so I didn't disturb them. It was only across the field at the back of the house, so I thought I'd go and check it out myself.

At the back of the field was a small group of trees, and I presumed that's where Lucy meant. I slipped out of the back gate and headed across the rain-soaked grass. I kept listening as I got closer, but I didn't hear anything that could be what Lucy described. Maybe she'd got it wrong, or this was the wrong place. I headed over there to check it out anyway.

As I got to the small copse, I think I did catch a glimpse of somebody. It was difficult to see as the bushes and undergrowth were high, so I continued on. As I moved round the outside of the trees, I saw it again. It did look like a hooman and it looked as though they glanced in my direction.

Now I heard them as well. They were definitely shouting at something, and I could see them swinging an arm as if they were striking out. This must be what Lucy meant, and I began to move forwards through the undergrowth.

I crept closer and closer until the man was almost in sight. Crawling behind some bushes, I thought if I peeped round, I should be able to see him. The hooman was still shouting as I moved nearer still. I slowly leant forwards, and was able to look into the small clearing where the hooman was.

That was it, I was there. I peered across at him, but the

sight that greeted me just filled me with confusion. The man was standing there, angrily shouting and swearing. He was swinging his arm with a branch in his hand. As he brought the branch down, he struck...a small cuddly toy.

As soon as I saw him, he looked straight at me. It was as if he knew I was there, or that I was coming. It suddenly became clear. Before I could move another muscle, I heard something from behind and then a small pin prick in my neck... then nothing.

Chapter 29
Cargo on Board

Stanley Gough turned the ignition in the old pickup truck and it spluttered into life. He walked over to the gate in the field and opened it, securing it with a large piece of concrete. He returned to the vehicle and drove across the wet field to the small group of trees at the far end. There, Bob Grimly was waiting for him.

'Come on.' said Grimly. 'This flipping dog weighs a tonne.'

Stanley Gough walked to the back of the pickup truck and lowered the tail gate. He then walked over to where his partner in crime was waiting. Together they lifted their huge, hairy cargo onto the back of the truck, and Gough closed the tail gate.

Both men were panting after the exertion of lifting the massive dog onto the vehicle.

'Let's go,' said Grimly. 'This stuff will wear off in about an hour and I definitely want to be back by then.'

The other man nodded in enthusiastic agreement and they both climbed into the truck's cab. A huge plume of dirty black smoke spurted from the rear of the truck as Stanley Gough started the vehicle and they drove back across the field and out through the open gateway.

Once on the road, he spared no time and pushed the ageing truck to its maximum speed. They had a 45-minute journey, so there was no time to waste.

When they reached Douglas Manor, Lord Devlin was

waiting for them. He ushered them to the stable block, and the truck spluttered to a halt at the main entrance. The men lifted the rear cover of the pick up to show their employer the spoils of their evil act.

'Excellent,' said Lord Devlin with his normal menacing tone. 'Now go and fetch the trolley. We need to help our guest settle into his accommodation.'

The two men went off for the trolley, sniggering.

Before long, they returned and Lord Devlin stood back while the two men loaded the trolley. They breathlessly pushed the cargo into the building and down to the vacant stable at the end.

'OK,' said Lord Devlin with even more threat in his voice, if that was possible. 'Let's get to work.'

CHAPTER 30
A PRISONER

When I slowly opened my eyes, everything was blurry, and I felt dizzy. Everywhere was dark and there was a musty, damp smell. My mind was frantically trying to piece together the previous events. I remembered heading over to the trees, and what Lucy had told me. Then it slowly started coming back to me. There was the man... and the toy... and then nothing. But I had realised something. It was a trap. I'd been tricked there by the man, and now I was here in the darkness.

As things became clearer, I tried to take in my surroundings. I tried to move, but there was something stopping me. My eyes were getting used to the dark now and I could see I was in a crate. It was only just big enough for me, so it was restricting how much I could move.

My mouth was sore and as I tried to open my jaws, I realised I couldn't. Something was stopping me and whatever it was, it was strong. I tried again, but I just couldn't open them at all. As well as my jaws, I had something wrapped around me like plastic. It was wrapped tightly round the bottom half of me and meant my back legs couldn't move.

As the minutes passed, I began to piece it all together. The man had tricked me into believing he was doing something nasty to a dog, but in reality, it was all made up. Then somebody else probably sneaked up behind me and injected me with something. I'd had enough needles recently to know that feeling.

I guess at that point it sent me to sleep, and I was moved to wherever I was now.

But where was I?

And who had done this to me?

My mind went back to the meeting with DOG and the guys from K9HQ – *'We have to assume that Growler has got the information about the incident from the Pomeranians. We must also assume that he now thinks you have the STOPnSLEEP and has reported that back to Devlin.'*

After all of my thoughts that the warning wasn't real, I was now beginning to seriously think that it was. What else could it be? The really worrying thing was that they appeared to know about the tracker, that must be why my jaws had been stopped from moving. Surely it was to stop me from barking and alerting the others to where I was.

So, I had to assume that I was being held captive, and that nobody knew where I was. If that was the case, this was really serious. But what was going to happen next? It wouldn't be long before I found out.

A short while later, I heard noises, possibly footsteps, and they were getting closer. Then there was the clanging of doors opening and the footsteps moved even closer. Suddenly, some fumbling and a door flew open. Light flooded into the room where I was and I had my first opportunity to really take in my surroundings.

I appeared to be inside some sort of shed with straw piled up at one end. On the wall there were a variety of what looked like dog leads, but I'd seen things like this before. They were from horses; I was in a stable.

As I'd thought I was in a crate and as I looked down I could clearly see what they'd done to me. I was securely wrapped in clear plastic that was bound tightly and closely to my body.

Next to the crate there was a small table, and this was the bit that worried me most. There was a variety of shiny instruments. Things that looked like they gripped, others that appeared to be for cutting. I got the feeling it wasn't a coincidence they were there.

I was in big trouble.

As the door opened three hoomans entered. I recognised one of them from the woods. He was the man pretending to hit the toy. One of the men appeared to be in charge and he spoke as he looked down at me in the crate. 'Well, I see you're awake, Monty. Or should I call you Mighty Monty?' He turned to the others as if to make sure they laughed at his attempt at humour.

Of course, they did and, satisfied he turned back to me.

'I hope that the accommodation is to your satisfaction.' This time the men needed no prompting, and they sniggered in unison.

'Well, please make yourself comfortable because you will be our guest for a while.' He sneered as he said the words, and the feeling I'd had earlier about being in trouble increased.

The man turned to the others. 'Well go and get our guest

some water, we can't have him getting thirsty can we?'

One of the men hurriedly went over and got a bottle from the side and filled it up from a tap just outside the door. It looked like something you'd have on the side of a rabbit cage. He fixed it to the crate near my head.

'There,' said the first man again. 'That should do nicely. I hope you like soup as well.' This again brought a forced laugh from the two men, as they made sure to keep on the good side of their employer.

That was the final thing he said as the men all turned and left the stable. They stood outside for a while as I heard one of the men ask a question. 'When will we be starting the, er, operation sir?'

He seemed to struggle with the right words to say but it certainly did nothing to make me feel better.

'Doctor Vengle has been called away on a job and won't be back until later,' replied his boss. 'Until then we just keep things as they are. Make sure he has food and water. We wouldn't want anything to happen to him...YET.'

His words sent an icy chill through my body. Think Monty, think. I had to do something, but I was struggling to come up with any kind of plan.

Just before they closed the door and returned me to the darkness and solitude, I saw a dog appear in the opening. The men were talking and appeared not to notice him as he looked across at me. He was a big dog but despite that he looked fearful.

Suddenly the man in charge shrieked at him. 'Growler, what

are you doing here? Get back to the barn until I call for you – NOW!'

The dog jumped and then disappeared just as the door was slammed shut, and the footsteps disappeared into the distance. So that was Growler then? The reason I was here and in this mess.

Chapter 31
Growler's Regret

Growler returned to the barn as ordered, but he was troubled. He had seen Monty in the stable and he knew the danger the big dog was in. He also realised the part he'd played in his capture and imprisonment. The dark feelings would not leave him. He thought about the dog that he used to be and the one he'd become.

Finally, after hours of the turmoil in his mind, he could stand it no longer. He had to act.

Dusk was descending on the grounds of the manor house as the large Akita dog made his way out of the barn. He moved as stealthily as was possible when you have neither size nor camouflage on your side. He passed the stable block and followed the hedgerow, heading down to the field that marked the boundary of Lord Devlin's land.

Despite his best attempt at concealment, he failed and Bob Grimly spotted him as he made his way to the boundary. He quickly summoned his associate, and they began to call to the dog in an attempt to get him to return.

Lord Devlin arrived as Growler began to make his way across the field. In his hand was the device the dog feared most, and he did not hesitate to use it. The effect of the shock could visibly be seen as it reached Growler's collar. The dog yelped and stumbled in obvious pain.

The men stood watching, fully expecting the dog to turn around, but he continued now at full speed. Again, the device was activated and again the result was the same. This time the big dog actually fell, but within seconds he was back on his feet and running towards the boundary of the property. This meant he was also out of range of the hideous shock collar.

Seeing what the dog was attempting to do the three men ran into the field. Despite the trauma the dog had endured at their hands, he was moving at speed. Lord Devlin stopped as he viewed the fleeing dog and raised the device again. This time as he pushed the button, there was no effect and Growler continued with his escape and quickly moved out of sight.

'Shall we get the car sir?' said Stanley Gough nervously.

'No,' replied the visibly angry Lord. 'We have more important things to worry about and besides that, he's served his purpose and he won't last long out there on his own. Leave him. He's history.'

With that, he turned and returned to the house with the two men trailing behind.

Outside Douglas Manor, the large dog crossed the quiet road. He went through a small gap in the hedgerow and into the woods. This should keep him out of sight, he thought. Once into the cover of the trees, he turned south and headed at speed... in the direction of Wigwam...

...and my house.

CHAPTER 32
PUTTING THINGS RIGHT

Molly and the others were worried. They hadn't seen me since this morning, and that was unusual. When I first got the superpower, I would wander off sometimes when I saw hoomans who needed the K9indness, but since the roofing incident we had all agreed that I shouldn't do that stuff alone. This meant that me being missing for so long, was making everyone nervous.

It was later in the afternoon when Lucy had asked Cookie how I'd done with the man in the woods. Obviously, she knew nothing about it, so asked Lucy for more information.

They had all gone over to the trees behind the field, but the only thing they found was a toy. There also looked like somebody had been driving over there, but they just thought it was the farmer. It was a dead end. They were no nearer to learning anything about where I had gone – until later that evening.

It was getting dark when Poppy heard a rustling sound at the back of the garden. Thinking it may be something fun to chase, she had gone to investigate, only to find a limping, dishevelled Akita coming through the bushes.

Poppy was startled by the presence of the big dog and let out two warning barks. Everyone ran into the back garden thinking maybe I'd returned. As they confronted Growler, he said he had information about me and then he recounted the whole story.

He told them of the way he'd left K9HQ, and how he'd been taken in by Lord Devlin. He spoke about the way he'd been treated and especially the use of the electric collar and how he'd been forced to get information about me.

Then he told them about where I was and what they were going to do to me. He said he wanted no part of it and wanted to make things right.

'Well, you've picked an odd way of making things right,' said Cookie angrily.

The others all joined in with their heated comments until suddenly Growler held up a big paw.

'Look, I know I've done wrong and I am happy to face the punishment, but we need to act if we're to save Monty. This can wait for another day. I understand why you're angry, but let's make this right first.'

The others couldn't help but agree and could see the reasoning behind the big dog's argument.

'OK…' said Cookie. 'But this isn't over, not by a long way.'

Growler just nodded and looked dejectedly down at the ground.

'Right,' said Molly defiantly. 'Let's go and rescue Monty. Listen closely everyone…'

She took control. She was the eldest and that gave her seniority plus she already had a plan.

'I will go to where Monty is being held. Cookie you can come with me.'

Cookie looked pleased about that but not so much when

Molly continued.

'Growler, you will be with us. You know where Monty is so that makes sense.'

Cookie glared at the big Akita with a look of unfinished business, but remained quiet.

'What about us?' asked Bailey.

'You and Poppy need to go to K9HQ. They have secured Monty so that he can't activate the tracker so they'll be unaware what's happened or where he is. Our first job will be to free Monty and activate it so then you can join us. OK?'

She looked at everyone for approval and they all nodded.

Growler stepped forward. 'I can be more help if I can get this collar off,' he said. 'If I'm spotted and I'm wearing this, I'll be no use. They know they can control me if I'm wearing this thing.'

Bailey picked up his ball that was laying on the lawn. 'I have an idea. Mini-hooman Thomas is in the kitchen. He is really kind and loves all animals. If I can get him outside you can ask him, you still have the ability to, right?'

The big dog nodded and Bailey went into the house with his ball. As soon as Thomas saw Bailey, he knew what he wanted. 'You want me to throw the ball little guy?'

Bailey ran out into the garden and the young boy followed. Once in the garden he saw the others – and the Akita.

'Hello there fella,' he said quietly. 'Are you lost?'

At this point Growler walked forward and looked up at

Thomas. Thomas then kneeled in front of the dog and gently held his face in his two hands and looked deep into his eyes.

'You want me to take this collar off, is that what you want?'

He reached round and unfastened the awful contraption, and released it from around Growler's neck.

'There,' he said. 'That's better. Hmm, this thing looks awful.' He examined the collar and then lay it down on the grass. 'Well, it's gone now.' Thomas stroked the dog, who looked up at him with gratitude in his eyes.

Suddenly there was a shout from inside the house. 'Thomas, it's dinner time!'

The boy gave him a last pat on the head and headed back into the house.

'OK,' said Molly, 'this is our chance; let's go. If Thomas tells the hoomans about Growler we need to not be here. They'll be fine once we're all home safe and sound.'

They quickly headed to the gate that led onto the field. They went through the opening before heading their separate ways.

'Good luck everyone,' said Molly. 'We're going to need it.'

CHAPTER 33
ALERTING K9HQ

Meanwhile, back at Douglas Manor, Lord Devlin had ordered the hounds to be let loose in the grounds. 'I want them covering every entrance!' he roared at his two nervous looking workers. 'If that dog comes back here, I want him caught, do you hear me?' The two men nodded obediently and left to carry out his orders.

Poppy and Bailey quickly reached the oak tree in the woods, but were having trouble finding the way in to K9HQ. It was about twenty minutes later when a tall, slim Dalmatian dog appeared from behind the tree. 'Can I help you?' she asked in a very official tone.

'Yes,' replied Poppy, 'we need to see DOG or St Bernard, or anybody who can help. It's about Monty he's in trouble.'

Almost immediately a door opened and the Dalmatian ushered them inside. When they got into the room, she left, but as she did she said, 'Wait here, somebody will be here very soon.'

The two spangles looked at each other nervously. 'I hope so,' said Bailey.

Meanwhile, Molly, Cookie and Growler were making slower progress as the journey was long and the Akita was still feeling the effects of the shocks he'd received earlier.

It was close to midnight when they arrived at the manor.

'I know it's late,' said Growler, 'but at least we'll have the cover of darkness and they may be off their guard a little.'

He led them around to the far side of the manor grounds.

'This entrance is not very well known,' he said, 'we should be able to sneak in here without being seen. It's only a short way to the stable block from here.'

Back at K9HQ, Molly and Bailey were telling the full story to Dog, St Bernard and Dr Gold, who listened with increasing concern.

'So, just let me be absolutely clear about this,' said DOG. 'Growler just appeared in your garden and offered to help. Nobody made him or asked him?'

Bailey and Poppy nodded.

Dog looked across at St Bernard and the two dogs looked confused.

'Did Growler say how Monty was?' The Doctor's voice was filled with worry.

'He said he'd been locked up in a crate and they'd taped his jaws together to stop him from activating the tracker. They'd also wrapped him up in plastic to stop him using the K9indness, but apart from that, he seemed OK. At least for now.' Bailey's voice expressed his own concern.

St Bernard spoke next. 'I know roughly where this place is. I think we should begin to head towards it until we have the exact location from the tracker. Hopefully Molly and the others can succeed. It's crucial now we find him. I'll get the rest of the team ready.'

He left hastily as they prepared themselves for the journey ahead.

CHAPTER 34
BANDIT AND COOKIE

Growler led Cookie and Molly through a very old and rarely-used gate. It was rusty and covered with ivy, and creaked as they opened it. The dogs all looked around nervously as it shattered the silence of the dark evening.

They moved forward cautiously, following Growler as he led them towards the stable block. Suddenly, as if out of nowhere, a large Foxhound appeared before them, blocking the path.

'Bandit!' said Growler in a surprised voice.

The foxhound snarled. 'I thought you'd come through here. I wanted to be the one to catch you.'

The dogs had history. Growler had been given the task of making the hounds angry and vicious so they would chase the foxes. This meant he wasn't nice to them and particularly Bandit, who was the leader of the hounds.

'Wait...' said Growler. 'Let me explain...'

The foxhound snarled again and drew his lips back, exposing his large teeth that seemed to glow in the darkness, 'Oh this will be good,' he said sarcastically.

Growler began to describe the events that made him treat the hounds the way he had.

'The collar was their way of controlling me,' he explained. 'If I didn't do what they wanted, they would use it over and over. In the end it would have killed me.'

Bandit looked unconvinced, so Growler continued.

'As soon as I saw they'd captured Monty and I knew what they were doing I left, and alerted these guys. Nobody made me, I just want to do the right thing.'

He looked across at Cookie and Molly for support, and they both nodded.

'The collar is gone now, look.' He turned sideways to show him. 'They have no control over me now, but they have Monty in that stable block, and they are going to do awful things to him if we don't stop them.'

He had explained everything enthusiastically and honestly, but the dog blocking the path still seemed uncertain about what to do, so Cookie stepped forward.

'I can't believe that such a strong and handsome hound such as yourself wouldn't want to do the right thing,' she said in a voice as sweet and kind as she could muster.

As she spoke, she attempted to flutter her eyelashes at Bandit, but she had brambles stuck in her fur all round her head and down as far as her eyelids, from the journey through the woods. Unfortunately, this made her attempt at looking lovingly at him appear like she was just blinking really fast.

Despite her strange eye movements, Bandit liked her. He didn't know what it was. Maybe it was the nettles and branches she was covered in, or maybe it was the fact that she had somehow managed to wrap lines of elastic slobber all round her muzzle. She was certainly his type of girl.

'Maybe...' she continued, 'when all this is over, we could go

for a walk together. That would be nice, wouldn't it?' This
time she didn't try the eyelashes again, but just sort of slid
a little closer to him and looked into his eyes.

Bandit struggled to find the words but eventually stuttered, 'Y..Yes, that would be n...n...nice. What do you want me to do?'

Growler stepped forward. 'We really need a distraction. Something to get them away from the stable block so we can sneak in and rescue Monty.'

Bandit didn't look at Growler as he replied, but instead, he looked straight at Cookie.

'Leave it with me,' he said softly. 'Consider it done.' With that, he turned and ran down towards the stable block.

'Wow,' said Molly, 'that was amazing. You sounded really convincing, like you meant it.'

'I did,' said Cookie, 'I meant every word. He's so cute.'

CHAPTER 35
OUT OF THE CRATE

I had been in the crate for hours and I'm not afraid to say I was worried. I had tried and tried to get free of the things that were stopping me moving or barking, but with no success. I was still trapped in a crate, in the dark and somewhere that I didn't know.

My fears weren't helped when I heard footsteps again. It was familiar, like the last time, and I was proven right when the door suddenly opened and this time four hoomans entered.

They seemed in a hurry, and the man who had obviously brought the instruments began to organise them one by one on the table. The same man as before who had seemed to be in charge, was shouting his instructions to the other three.

'Quickly, get the equipment ready. Have you got the syringe and collecting vessel?' The man at the table nodded as if the questioning was annoying him.

'Get him out of that crate and ready for the procedure.' This instruction was to the other two men, and it filled me with dread. What was going to happen next?

The men opened the crate and began to try to lift me out. They found it a challenge, as the door was quite small and I was making it as difficult as possible by squirming and wriggling.

'Argghh, pack it in,' said one of the men, as I managed to

trap his hand between me and the crate entrance. I pushed as hard as I could before he managed to free his hand and drop me.

'Stop messing about,' said Lord Devlin with growing annoyance at the men's incompetence.

'We need to get him out, can we sedate him?' He looked across at the man at the table.

'No,' he replied, 'I need him fully conscious to be able to do the procedure.'

Obviously concerned by their boss's anger, the two men grabbed me again and this time managed to get me out of the crate. Now I just lay there, unable to move my back legs or open my mouth. It seemed I was powerless to stop whatever was going to happen to me.

Suddenly, there was a huge commotion from outside. The air was filled with the sound of hounds baying and there seemed like a lot of them. It was obvious something was happening, and the men were startled and concerned.

'It must be Growler!' said Lord Devlin, sounding extremely agitated.

'He must be back and he might not be alone. You stay here and get this done. No more delays!' His orders were directed at Doctor Vengle. He then turned to the other two men. 'You two with me – NOW!'

They immediately stopped what they were doing and followed in his wake.

I lay there waiting for the inevitable as the man prepared his gruesome instruments.

Chapter 36
A Rescue Party

Outside the kennel block the three rescuers had heard the hounds and hurried towards the entrance.

'That's our distraction,' said Growler, 'let's hope it's worked.'

Growler led them through the door and up to the end stable where he had seen Monty in the crate. When they got there they peered quietly through the door. There at the back of the small stable was Dr Vengle. He had his back to them and was kneeling down. Just to the side of him, they spotted me.

They ducked back out and Growler whispered to the others, 'That's the one who is going to try and get the K9indness. We have to stop him somehow.'

'I have an idea,' said Cookie, and the three gathered round to listen as she spoke.

Inside, I'd seen them at the door. My hearing luckily wasn't affected by the restraints and I'd heard them approach and now listened as they made their plans. Suddenly, the man stood up. I knew he needed to be kneeling for the rescue attempt, so I wriggled and struggled just as much as I could. He immediately resumed his position next to me and held me still.

'Relax...' he sneered. This won't take lon...'

He never managed to get the words out before he was hit at full speed from behind by Cookie and Growler.

The force and speed at which they slammed into him took him totally by surprise and smashed him straight into the wall.

He fell face down, stunned and, for now, immobilised. The two big dogs now leapt onto his back and attempted to keep him held down.

'Quick Molly!' said Cookie, 'Now!'

With that, Molly ran over to me and began to tear at the tape holding my jaws together. As she chewed at them, she was keeping up an endless commentary.

'At last, I can use my superpower. Eat anything I can. Anything. And never get sick.'

Despite all the chatter, she made short work of the tightly wound fastening and with one last nibble it came off.

It was an amazing feeling to be free after all this time and I opened my mouth to stretch my aching jaw.

'Bark!' yelled Cookie. I looked over at her and she repeated her instruction. 'Bark! You know three times to get the tracker going!'

In the commotion of the rescue, I had totally forgotten about it but now I let out three loud barks.

WOOF! WOOF! WOOF!

Meanwhile, Molly went to work on the plastic wrapped around my back legs and rear end. She continued talking about her superpower, though I was really hoping she wasn't eating this stuff.

Suddenly, her collar began to flash and beep loudly. Of course, I had activated the tracker and now it was noisily announcing my location.

This seemed to arouse the fallen hooman, who began to struggle under the weight of the two dogs.

'I can't hold him much longer,' said Growler.

Molly still hadn't fully released me, so Cookie looked across at him.

'Again?' she said. Instantly, Growler knew what she meant, and they both jumped off the man and went back to the door. He drowsily began to get up, now free from the weight that had been holding him down. He slowly got back to his knees and this was the signal for the second charge. Again, they hit the man and again he went down. Jumping on his back, Cookie looked across at Molly.

'Carry on Molly, let's get Monty free.'

It only took a few minutes before all the restraints had gone. I walked over to the fallen hooman and looked at Cookie and Growler.

'OK, you can get down now. I've got this.'

WOOSH!

As he raised his head, he looked around in confusion. I hit him with two fierce blasts of K9indness and he coughed to confirm success.

'Come on…' I said. 'He won't be troubling us again.'

There was a point I never thought I'd escape the crate and stable, but I had. Thanks to Molly, Cookie and Growler, I was finally free.

There was no time to congratulate ourselves though; there was work to be done.

Chapter 37
Grimly and Gough Running Scared

Outside, the three men had been following the baying hounds around the grounds... and around... and around... and around. Finally, Lord Devlin realised things were not as they seemed.

'Back to the stables!' he ordered the men. 'Make sure Vengle is doing what I'm paying him for. I'm going to the house to get us an extra deterrent, just in case anybody thinks of trying anything stupid.'

Bob Grimly and Stanley Gough entered the stable block as instructed. Once through the main door, they began to head down to the end and that's when we emerged.

At first, they looked shocked, but that quickly turned to panic as they realised they were probably in big trouble. Growler led as we ran towards the two men. He had been mistreated by them for so long that he now wanted to even the score.

Now free from the collar that had been used to control him, the Akita picked up speed as he got closer. Molly, Cookie and I were close behind and we must have seemed a terrifying sight to these two cowardly hoomans. Like the bullies they were, now that the odds were a little more even, all of a sudden, they were not quite so brave.

One look at each other, and they turned and ran. This was a race though that they were never going to win. As we got closer, they suddenly veered off to the right and leapt

over the stable door of an empty cubicle. The bottom
half of the door was closed and so the two terrified men
thought they would be safe.

Looking around the stable passageway we saw an empty
feed box that we easily pushed to the stable door. The
two men had retreated to the back of the stable and were
trying to raise help on their phones. I climbed onto the box
and turned round so I was facing away from the men.

I looked at the others. 'How many? What do you think?'

'About six,' said Molly, 'best to make sure.'

I smiled. 'Six it is then.'

The two men were yelling and shouting now. All I could
hear was, 'We're sorry! He made us do it!'

I ignored them as I delivered six large blasts of K9indness
and wafted it straight at them with my tail.

WHOOSH! WHOOSH! WHOOSH!

WHOOSH! WHOOSH! WHOOSH!

I quickly nudged the open top of the stable door with my
nose and it slammed shut. We stood outside and listened to
them as they spluttered in the confined stable.

Bailey, Poppy and the K9HQ rescue team were close by
when the receiver they were carrying began to bleep.
They made their way quickly into the manor grounds, past
the huge pack of foxhounds who greeted them warmly.

Bandit approached the group. 'Follow me,' he said, 'I'll show you where they are'.

Lord Devlin had fetched his shotgun from the house and was busily loading it as he saw the four dogs leaving the stable block. He hadn't gone through all of this bother to have it ruined now, he thought, as he headed straight towards the group.

CHAPTER 38
THE FINAL SHOWDOWN

We saw the nasty hooman as we came out of the stable block. He had seen us too, but he didn't look like he was going to run. As we got closer, we saw something in his hand and he lifted it up and pointed it towards us. Growler had seen this many times as he had been forced to accompany the Lord and his guests when they went out shooting animals around the manor

'Get down!' shouted Growler loudly as the shot rang out.

We managed to get into cover and we heard a loud crack strike somewhere to the side of us. Again, the man raised the gun and again the noise filled the air. We were trapped, and he knew it. He reloaded and began to march towards us.

Suddenly, he stopped and seemed to look past us into the distance. As we turned, we saw the whole pack of foxhounds charging towards where we were. With them were pretty much the whole of K9HQ.

The noise was deafening as they barked, howled, and bayed. The man was clearly unsettled by the sight as he began to retreat. However, instead of turning away he backed up slowly, raising the gun. Again, he fired and again he took aim while walking backwards toward the house.

He was now at the path that went along the top of the yard outside the manor house when, all of a sudden, I spotted something on the path beyond him. Bailey and

Poppy had sneaked around him and were now directly in his path as he walked backwards.

We needed to keep him looking this way because I think I knew what they had planned. Directly below where Lord Devlin was retreating was the biggest pile of farmyard manure you've ever seen. It was about ten feet high and you could smell it in the nearby village when the wind was in the right direction.

Everybody was under cover now, but I needed to distract him. I ran from behind the small shed where I was hiding and began to bark loudly as I charged forward.

The man spotted me and raised the gun so it was pointing straight at me. As he pulled the trigger, the shot flew straight over my head, in fact way over my head.

I heard the shot as it hit way up on the top of the barn behind us, and then the reason became clear. As Lord Devlin was about to take his shot, he stepped backwards and began to lose his balance. He had tripped over something and was falling. His gun flew from his hands as he fell... straight into the stinking manure pile below.

Bailey and Poppy looked at each other. It had worked.

Everybody arrived at the scene at the same time. We were all crowded onto the path above the manure pile. I looked down and saw the sorry looking hooman almost up to his neck in steaming, stinking putrid manure and it was a wonderful sight.

Everyone was congratulating each other and celebrating the demise of Lord Devlin, but I knew I still had work to do.

I moved around the wall until I was directly above him.
He was shouting and yelling commands and orders that
nobody was taking any notice of. I just heard him yell, 'Do
you know who I am?!' as I got into position and blasted a
succession of K9indness servings.

I don't know how many there were. I just wanted to make
sure they hit the target. My tail swept them down to Lord
Devlin and his cough was like music to my ears.

After trying so hard to gain control of a superpower, the
evil hooman had finally received one, just not in the way
that he'd planned.

Honey, I mean, Doctor Gold, was the first to get to me once I'd dealt with Lord Devlin.

'Are you OK?' she said, with genuine concern in her voice. 'I heard what they did to you, those awful hoomans. I can't believe I, er we, could have lost you.'

'I'm fine,' I assured her, 'my rescue was never in doubt, not with this team. They're all superheroes.' I looked across at Cookie, Bailey, Poppy and Molly. The hounds had surrounded them and they were having a great time telling their stories of heroism.

I heard later that Bailey and Poppy had asked DOG if they could become superheroes.

'We already have a name,' said Bailey. Then both together they said 'Trip Hazard!'

I don't know how that one's going.

Cookie and Bandit were making plans to take that walk together. Maybe not in the woods, though, they agreed.

Growler walked slowly over to me as everyone began to disperse. His head was bowed and he continued to look at the ground as he spoke.

'I'm ready,' he said, with a tremor in his voice.

'Ready for what?' I replied.

'For the K9indness. I realise how selfish I've been. I caused all of this. It's my fault.'

'Look at me Growler,' I said, and the big dog raised his head.

'You don't need the K9indness my friend, you already had it. You just needed to find it inside yourself.'

Chapter 39
What Became of the Baddies?

We can't leave this story without telling you what happened to Lord Devlin, his two workers and the evil vetandhairyman can we?

Well, Lord Devlin became one of the most respected and kind men in the whole country. He used his position and influence to become a supporter of animal rights. He fought against illegal hunting and opened Douglas Manor to the public. The grounds were always full of people walking their dogs and children playing on the free adventure park that Lord Devlin had built.

The hounds had a brand-new kennel block, and no longer had to chase foxes. Instead, they enjoyed their exercise around the grounds and Bandit especially liked it when a certain bramble-covered Newfydoof came to visit.

Bob Grimly and Stanley Gough continued to work for the Lord but instead of organising awful things against animals, they ran the pet farm that rescued neglected animals from all over the country.

Doctor Vengle looked after all the animals at Douglas Manor as well as volunteering for an animal charity.

Growler was hired by DOG in a consultancy role – for now. His first job was to tell our hoomans the whole story. It will probably help them understand their disappearing dogs.

Me? Well, I went back to my kind of normal life with the hoomans, spangles and Cookie.

I was still Mighty Monty though, and I carried
on with my work changing the world, I guess,
one FART at a time.

THE ALMOST END...

It was about six months after the Lord
Devlin incident that I was relaxing in the garden.

All of a sudden, I heard, 'Psst Monty...'

I turned round to see St Bernard in the gateway
at the bottom of the garden. He looked worried.

'How would you like
a trip on a plane?

We have a problem...

A big one.'

THE REAL END

MEET THE STARS OF THE BOOK

LEFT TO RIGHT - POPPY, MOLLY, BAILEY

COOKIE

WE HOPE YOU ENJOYED THIS BOOK!

If you'd like to see more
from the author, visit:
www.montydogge.com

If you'd like to see more
from the illustrator, visit:
www.whimsicolourart.com